"Let the gal go!" the big man yelled.

Ryder's arm drew back, roundhoused forward to slam a fist solid as a chunk of granite to his adversary's jaw. The fellow's grip on the girl relaxed and she twisted away. Taking his cue, Ryder waded into the hardcase's midsection.

One, two, three solid punches to his gut and chest flung the roughneck back against the corral. Groggy, the man tried to pull his long-barreled Remington Navy Model. Ryder grabbed his shirt and spun him around.

Hot lead intended for Ryder tore into the hardcase and he fell limp. Clawing the gun from the corpse's hand, Ryder cocked, crouched and shot in a single motion. The bearded giant of a man riding down on Ryder flung both arms up, shrieked, and fell.

RYDER
#2: LONGHORN SISTERS

COLE WESTON

Ivy Book
Published @ Ballantine Books

Copyright © 19?? by Butterfield Press, Inc.

All rights reserved under International and Pan-American Copyright Conventions. Published in the United States by ...

IVY BOOKS • NEW YORK

Ivy Books
Published by Ballantine Books

Produced by Butterfield Press, Inc.
133 Fifth Avenue
New York, New York 10003

Library of Congress Catalog Card Number:86-91838

ISBN 0-8041-0017-9

Manufactured in the United States of America

First Edition: May 1987

LONGHORN SISTERS

CHAPTER 1

"Son of a bitch! Lame!"

The big man on the rangy bay gelding stretched in the saddle, then swung down and stood grim faced beside his animal under the vast Texas sky. The horse had been favoring his off foreleg and had finally stumbled. Not a good spot for this to happen: towns, even ranches in the region were widely placed, and a long, footsore hike seemed in store for any so unfortunate as to be caught out here without a mount. Still, at least it was white man's country, and one needn't be overmuch concerned there'd be run-ins with redskins, as in the Indian Nation farther north or the Staked Plains, many days' ride toward the setting sun.

Under the brim of his stetson, the man's eyes glittered as they surveyed the empty horizon. Parched grassland, baked by summer sun, swept away in all directions, stove-top flat and radiating stove-like stifling heat.

The man dropped to one knee to inspect that foreleg. As he did, one hand swept automatically to adjust the foot-and-a-half-long scabbard slung

1

at his waist, from the top of which protruded the burnished handle of a cavalry sabre.

He was tall, a shade above six-foot-two, and carried his thirty-two years easily on shoulders as powerful and broad as a heavyweight boxer's. Long, sun-burnished brown hair curled over his collar. He had medium-length sideburns and a full, trimmed mustache.

Now he fished in the pocket of his leather vest and brought out a lucifer match, which he thrust stick first between straight, white teeth. Habit. "Well, horse," he bit out around the match, "that dry gully where you slipped looks like it done it for you. You'll be all right after some days to heal, but today you can't carry me. Won't ask you to."

Andrew Ryder rose to his full height, looped the reins in the crook of his elbow and began to walk west, in the direction of Yorktown, his destination before the sudden forced halt.

Yorktown—a place he'd never visited, yet which had many strong associations for Ryder. It was the town near the one his Holly's pa had planned, all those years ago before the War, to buy land. Before Ryder's lovely and vibrant bride-to-be had been raped by renegades, then had committed suicide. Before the old man, shot by the same bunch, had died in Ryder's arms after relating the story.

It was sobering to actually be in the region for the first time. Although Ryder hadn't laid eyes on it till now, it seemed familiar due to Randolph Fawcett's excited description eight years earlier. The old-timer, sitting in a rocker on his front porch overlooking the farm outside Atlanta, had said, "Texas, Andrew! Texas! It's a fresh and brawling slice of God's country, and land there is cheap as a whore's promise. Why, I aim to quadruple my acreage and never look back at this worn-out red-dirt farm!" And Holly had been happy anticipating the spring wedding, to be followed by the move west with her pa and new husband, the tall, straight and handsome Andrew Ryder.

That had been before Fort Sumter. At the outbreak of the War Between the States, Ryder had enlisted with the rebel cause. And then had come Antietam . . . Gettysburg . . . Chickamauga. It had been at this last battle that Ryder, beside a stream that flowed blood-red, snapped his sabre against a Yankee bayonet . . .

Now Ryder brushed sweat from his brow with a shirtsleeve, doggedly maintaining his pace at the head of the lame horse. His fingers plucked chewed lucifer from his lips, snapped the brittle wood and tossed the pieces. "Come on, boy."

Sundown edged the ragged clouds with fire, the orange sky was quickly darkening. Time to think of bedding down.

Ryder made dry camp that night on the rim of a wash. Although it didn't look like rain, the big man, as always in this type of country, was leery of flash flooding. Head cradled in his grounded stock saddle, he spent the moments before sleep watching the star-diamonds on the night's black velvet curtain, recalling recent events. Driving a longhorn herd north to Lone Tree. No market drive this, but a restocking effort for a rancher named

3

Bannemann, whose herd had been decimated by rustlers. Now the Blaine gang were all hanged for their thieving ways, and a recovered cash stash had paid for replacement San Antone beef on the hoof. They'd been driven north nice and easily by a crack crew, including Ryder.

The ramrod, on paying the drovers off, had returned south. The boys had drunk a lot, gambled some, fought a little in the cowtown saloons of Lone Tree before breaking up to go their separate ways. Ryder had kept most of his bankroll intact by steering clear of the beckoning card games. He'd wanted most to be gone from this region fraught with reminders of Holly Fawcett. But there was still Yorktown to ride through before making the clean break for New Mexico Territory . . .

He slept, with distant coyote cries serving as his lullaby.

In the dream, Ryder was witnessing Holly's rape. The images were vivid, thanks to old Fawcett's descriptions. Ten men, some dressed in blue, some in gray, surrounded the young woman: In the last days of the War, the bunch had grouped as ruthless renegades not for the Northern cause or the Southern, but for themselves, to burn and pillage the length of ruined, burned-out Georgia. The dregs of both armies, they stood clutching their bulging groins through trouser fabric. The girl, blonde and petite, had been stripped naked; she stood on slender legs, her body trembling, full, rose-tipped breasts goose-bumped from fear.

"Who'll go first?"

4

"Who d'you reckon?" This speaker wore a Confederate sergeant's blouse, the original butternut color streaked now with grime. The leader snarled, "Zeke! Lucius! Pin her!" Two renegade bluebellies threw the girl to the ground, stretched her arms above her head and sat on them as her horrified father watched. The one pinning her right side had only one eye, and a jagged scar angled from right cheek to hairline.

The "sergeant" thrust his pants down, dropped to his knees . . .

Ryder woke in a sweat. He seldom dreamed at all, and hadn't for years been plagued with this one based on Holly's pa's account. Now he sat up to confront the pre-dawn glow in the eastern sky. *Must be this country I'm riding through,* he thought. *Damn it to hell! No sense to it, none at all.*

The horse's leg still appeared swollen, incapable of safely carrying much extra weight. After a quick breakfast of jerky and cracked corn washed down with a splash of canteen water, Ryder saddled up but didn't mount. He led out, planting one worn army boot in front of the other in a steady, mile-eating pace. The limping bay trailed at the end of the reins.

Ryder spotted the smoke about mid-morning, dead ahead and beyond a ridge unusual in that it was topped by a fringe of brush. Water was near. The gelding sensed it too, as evidenced by pricked-forward ears and an excited urge to move ahead faster. "Easy," Ryder told the animal. From the top of the rise he could see it all: a small ranch with pole corral, barn, bunkhouse, sheds and privies laid out along the banks of a small creek. The main house, basically an overgrown cabin, showed a few stylish touches: shutters, a veranda with flanked laddering, rose trellises. A half-dozen cow ponies occupied the corral. No humans were in sight.

A place to lay over and let the bay rest, Ryder calculated. The trailing wages in his money belt would enable him to pay for bed and food. Or, if such turned out to be the owner's wish, the big man didn't mind putting hands to a few days' honest toil.

Ryder grinned and the mustache bristled at the corners of his mouth. He tugged the bay's reins and started down the slope.

He allowed the horse to drink at the creek nearer the house as he stood patiently, scanning this modest spread's layout again. On the acreage beyond the buildings, cattle were scattered to graze. But not many cattle, and only scant graze. There were no hands in sight. Maybe they'd gone to town, or to some roundup activity going on in a remote draw. All in all, Ryder had no reason to suspect danger, and yet the hairs on his neck tingled uncomfortably. The gray eyes narrowed; his right hand drifted toward his six-gun.

The shot boomed without warning and a geyser of dirt erupted close to Ryder's boot. Too close! Slapping the bay's rump to spook him, the big man simultaneously powered to his left, sidelonging toward a bulky patch of sage. A second rifle report and a third rang out, as fast as the marksman could jack fresh shells into the repeater's chamber. Ryder hit the earth rolling and clawed the .45 Model Smith & Wesson Schofield from its well-worn holster. Sun glittered wickedly from the bright nickel plating.

"Clear out, mister! Just you mount up that cayuse and clear out!" The voice on the clear air was high-pitched, like a boy's, and apparently came from the window in the front of the house from which a moment before plumes of gunsmoke had been billowing. "You hear me, mister?"

"I hear you!" Ryder's own shout covered the forty-yard distance to the sprawling, unpainted structure.

"What you doing here?" A damned funny question, it seemed to Ryder. Hadn't this outfit ever had a traveler stop for water, or to rest a lame mount before? The folks in the house had to figure him for a bad actor, pinning him down this way. He glanced to his left, right, and over his shoulder back up the slope. Beyond the declivity in which he hunkered lay open ground, and the way things stood, it looked like an invitation to sudden death to try and move. The house was beyond effective six-gun range, and his Winchester remained aboard the bay that had now wandered down beside the creek.

"I said, what you doing here at the Rocking K?"

"Just passing through this country," Ryder shouted. "My horse lamed up a piece back, and I was fixing to ask some help here."

"You ain't Robeson's man?"

"Never heard of anybody name of Robeson!"

COLE WESTON

"Prove it!"

"I'll prove my story about a lame cayuse. Take a
look at the bay by the creek. Favoring his leg, sure
as shooting." In a run-in against true hardcases he
could be counted on as the grim killing machine
the War had made him, thriving on danger, totally
alive in the face of death. For example, maybe in a
case like this he'd charge with a blazing six-gun. It
had worked for him more than once in the past,
with heavy loss of life the result. But the way this
standoff was shaping up, the one in the house was
some shavetail ranch kid who'd likely been ordered by his pa to defend the place. Ryder didn't
cotton to gunning innocent ranch folk, especially
young'uns. "Look, come on outside and let's both
do some explaining. There's no call for blood-
shed."

The voice inside said, "You heard that, Jess.
What do you think?" The response was so soft that
Ryder couldn't catch it. But after a moment the
call came: "We're coming out!"

And so they did, to Ryder's amazed eyes. A tall,
redheaded young woman stepped through the door
and onto the porch, a Henry carbine cradled in her
slender arms. Her legs were cased in tight jeans,
and pointed breasts prodded the cambray fabric of
her man's shirt.

But there was more. A pleasingly plump blonde
stepped forth, similarly attired in man's garb. This
one's bosom was more rounded and ample, her
shirt stretched to straining by twin muskmelon-
size globes. "Come on, Jessica," she called over a
shapely shoulder.

By now Ryder was standing beside the sage clump with the Smith & Wesson holstered, hands raised to chest level to show innocence of purpose. The stunning figures of the women made his jaw drop with surprise. All along he'd figured the high voice belonged to a kid.

"Jess! Damnation! Get yourself out here!" The redhead sounded as if she'd lost all patience.

A third female appeared, tiny in the doorway, and this one had on a thin gingham dress. She was doll-like in size and perfection of form, with creamy skin and sleek thighs outlined through the cloth. Her hair was raven-black and surrounded her face in a mass of inky waves.

A beautiful face, more beautiful than . . . Wait—the redhead's high cheekbones and firm chin presented . . . no, the perfect heart-shaped face of the blonde got the nod from a *true* fancier of lovely ladies.

But all three faces were sternly frowning. Finally the blonde declared, "Better wipe that grin off'n your puss, mister. Liz, here, has already pumped bullets into one horny hombre since our husbands got carried off with lead poisoning."

It went a long way toward explaining the situation here at the Rocking K. "Ladies, I'm real sorry to hear about your departed menfolk. When accidents—"

"Accidents, my ass," the redhead called Liz hissed, blue eyes blazing. "Joe, Jack, Jamie, not a one of the brothers got took by accident. Call it by its right name, if you call it anything! Cold-blooded murder!"

9

CHAPTER 2

Ryder stood for a silent thirty or forty seconds in the dust of the ranch yard, watching the three women, studying on what the one called Liz had just said. The way he understood it, three men, brothers, had recently died and there was suspicion of foul play. And if the men had been the husbands of the pretty trio on the porch, the gals had cause aplenty to be edgy about a stranger who'd just ridden in. In fact, he was probably luckier than he knew not to have been tagged by a bullet before now.

It must be his honest face.

"Like I was saying, ladies, I'm plumb sorry to hear three good men are dead." He was assuming the men had been good because these three had married them. He went on with his sympathetic speech. "If murder was what happened, that's got to add to your pain. If you want to talk about it, I'm willing to listen. If you say you don't want me on your land, I'll take my lame horse and hike on out of here."

"Just a minute." Liz gestured at her two companions on the porch and the women huddled to converse in whispers. Ryder stood at ease. Although the redhead cradled the Henry so its muzzle pointed in his direction, he felt safe—if he didn't try and close distance on them. But he wasn't shy of moving. As was his habit in times of waiting, he brought a lucifer out of his vest pocket, thrust the stick end in his mouth. For a man who scorned tobacco, it was something to do.

At last the females broke up their parley. As they faced him now, they still appeared tense, but noticeably less so. "You don't know Richard Robeson, you claim?"

Ryder shook his head. "Never heard of the feller. I told you before."

"I'm inclined to believe him," Liz told the others. "Robeson wouldn't have sent one hardcase out here, but a dozen. And if this feller is a decoy, the real attack from behind would have started by now. This man—say, what's your name, anyhow?"

"Ryder."

"Girls, I didn't keep Ryder, here, covered too sharp just in order that if there were sidekicks lurking about they could make their play. Nobody did."

"So, what now, Liz?" the brunette queried. Her gaze held hotly on the big man.

"Aw, hell. Go catch your mount, Ryder, and fetch him over to the stable and put him up. Meantime, me and the girls'll boil some coffee. You look like you could use some to wash the trail dust out of your gullet."

He grinned. "I reckon I do."

The women disappeared inside, and Ryder went after the bay. He caught the gelding after about ten minutes, most of the time spent hiking to the bend in the creek where the animal stood cropping grass.

The trouble came inside the barn.

When Ryder led the horse through the big doors his eyes had to adjust; the outside glare was brutal this late in the morning. In the half-light he made out a half-dozen grain sacks stacked against the wall, and beyond, a row of empty stalls. Unsaddling swiftly, he turned the bay into the first stall and picked up a pitchfork to toss in hay from a broken bale in a corner. As he was bent over, a shadow in the next stall thickened and moved, but it was too late for Ryder to go for his gun. A weighted whipstock was already swinging in an overhand arc and met Ryder's head hard.

When he came to, Ryder knew only one sensation: pain. His arms were wrenched, his legs stretched taut, and his head throbbed powerfully where behind his ear a gash still trickled blood. But there was no feeling in his hands. Lengths of stout hemp piggin cord had been half-hitched around his wrists to hold him spread-eagled on his back in the middle of the barn floor. Each limb was snubbed to a stanchion, just as if he were a hog readied for slaughter. The thin spread of hay he lay on might have been comfortable but for his fix; he was fully clothed, the prickly stem ends effectively blunted. But he couldn't move more than an inch in any direction, and when he tried he simply loosed stampeding pain. There seemed to be nothing to do but wait.

He figured one of the three vixens must have sneaked in here when he'd been chasing down the bay. No other explanation made sense. Hidden, she'd come at him with her club while his hands were full. Damn! He wasn't fooled often, but once was enough!

Still, he was alive . . .

After what seemed like hours, Ryder heard approaching footfalls. When he craned his neck he saw the women, Liz in the lead, still toting the Henry carbine, and the dark Jessica at her side as they strode in and directly up to him.

"What's keeping Cathy?"

"She'll be here."

Ryder was getting the names straight, if a bit belatedly. He'd heard the redhead called Liz; she was the oldest, although if she owned so many as twenty-six or -seven winters he'd eat his stetson. The black-haired beauty, Jess, was at least five years shy of her sister-in-law, and she and blond Cathy looked to be of an age. All three seemed spooked as hell—they had to be, behaving this way. Cold-cocked as he was putting up his horse. Jesus! And now tied!

"Little Miss Fancypants," Liz snorted. "She didn't get *that* much of this jasper's blood on her."

Jess shrugged. "You know Cathy. Likes to wash."

Ryder looked up at the pair. Damn, but the black-hair had fine ankles below her skirt-hem. He cleared his throat and said, "The blonde is the one who laid for me?"

"My orders." Liz shifted her rifle to the crook of her arm. "Since I was the oldest of the Kennesaw brothers' wives, a lot of the leadership around the Rocking K fell on me. Then, when our menfolk got picked off one by one, and with the other girls a bit shy about ordering punchers around, I more or less got stuck with the boss role. Jessica and Cathy lean on me, but I'm weaning them. That's why all of us are going to be here together when we decide what to do with you."

"Why do anything? Why not just let me lead my horse on out and off into the sunset?"

"Ha!"

"Ha!" the black-haired woman echoed. "Say, though, Liz, what would be wrong in doing like he says? You said yourself it really don't look much like he's Robeson's man."

"There's appearance and then there's for-damn-sure truth of matters, little sister," Liz observed. "That's why we're going to hold our war council on Mr. — "

"Ryder," he reminded her.

"Mr. Ryder. Whether to turn him loose or over to the law. Ah, here's Cathy now."

A shadow fell across Ryder's face as the plump blonde lovely flounced through the barn door and drew up beside the others standing over him. The woman called Cathy was so ravishingly beautiful with that oval face and bountiful bosom and all, that he could hardly hold it against her, the fact she'd clubbed him from behind—or that her blond hair reminded him of his poor Holly. She even

15

looked kind of sorry her sister-in-law had put her up to the foul deed.

"Are we ready?"

"Ready as we'll ever be." Cathy glanced down at Ryder and her eyes lingered on the bulge at his crotch.

"Then let's vote." Authority bristled in Liz's voice. For all her speechifying on truth, was it true that she scorned the leader's part? Ryder couldn't tell for sure.

"All in favor of shooting the jasper where he lies?"

"Hey! Wait a minute!"

Liz's rifle barrel dug Ryder's ribs. "You hush up, Ryder! Well, girls?"

Jess and Cathy kept arms resolutely pressed down at their sides, voting no. Ryder exhaled in relief.

"For turning him loose?"

The dark-haired Jessica's slender hand fluttered upward, though hesitantly.

Liz fixed her with a glare. "Remember, Richard Robeson wants this ranch. It stands in the way of his own spread's expansion to more water. After our men turned down Robeson's buy-out offers, they died."

Jessica's hand bolted into her dress pocket.

Liz smiled down at the spread-eagled man with fake sweetness. "Her vote was merely one against our two, Ryder. You wouldn't have been set free anyhow, never mind my speech."

"Obliged for your explanation."

But Liz wasn't paying attention to Ryder's

words, much less his sarcasm.

"The other choice we have, girls, is to get the opinion of Lemuel. All in favor?" Jess's and Cathy's hands shot up. Liz's followed as she nodded satisfaction. "Lemuel is checking brands today down by the south line. As for who'll ride there to find him—"

"I'll go!"

"All right, Cathy. You're dressed for it, at least, and can start right off." She glanced disapprovingly at Jessica's ruffled dress, then back toward the big-chested blond. "Take Rambunction."

"That's *your* mare!"

"She's fast. Bring Lemuel back with you. Tell him about Mr. Ryder, here. Do you need help saddling up?"

"Of course not!"

"Then get going. Rambunction is in the corral. You can throw a loop on her without much trouble. Jessica?"

"Yes, Liz?"

"When Cathy rides out I'm going up to the house. Take this." She thrust the Henry she'd been carrying around ever since Ryder first laid eyes on her into Jessica's milk-white, satin-smooth hands. "You stay in the barn and keep watch over Ryder. I've had me a long, hot day and deserve a bath and nap. For once I'm going to treat myself." The brunette handled the weapon less familiarly than her sister-in-law. "What'll I do if he tries to escape?"

The redhead laughed. "*Try* is all he's likely to do! I tied those ropes myself. But if he squirms loose, use the rifle. And not just to clobber him, either. Shoot to kill."

With that Liz spun on her heel, linked arms with the blonde Cathy and stalked out. As they crossed the wide threshold, the tall redhead whispered to her companion, drawing a lilting giggle.

For a while there was the noise of hoofbeats as Cathy cut Rambunction apart from the other horses in the corral, but eventually this quieted too and a deep summer morning silence descended, broken only by flies buzzing around fresh manure. Ryder shook his head vigorously, hoping somehow to diminish the ache, and failing. Now he fixed his gaze on his guard, and he'd rarely been left helpless near a more lovely-to-look-at sight. Jessica Kennesaw had planted her trim bottom on a hay bale near the stanchion to which Ryder's left foot was snubbed, and held the carbine slackly across her lap. The woman's bright eyes were a pale aquamarine color, and they peered back at the prisoner steadily, and unless he missed his guess, with curiosity as well. Nothing Liz had said amounted to proof he was an agent of their rancher foe, Robeson, and Jessica seemed aware of this. Ryder sensed a note of sympathy.

It was a long time after the other women had gone that Jess murmured, "Ryder, you're called. Do you have a first name?"

He lifted his head so as to look directly at her. "It's Andrew. Nobody uses it, though. Not for a long time."

"Uh huh. You were in the War, I reckon. Something to do with that?"

"Yes."

"Do you wonder how I guessed? About your past?" Ryder tried to shrug, but found his bonds limited him too much. So he simply lay still.

"It's the sword scabbard. Officers carried them. My daddy had a picture, and him and the other Confederate officers all were wearing swords, but longer than yours. I recognized the kind of handle."

Ryder nodded. He saw now that his weapons belt was in the woman's hands. Suddenly, as if on impulse, she grasped the burnished brass sabre handle and drew the weapon it was attached to from its sheath. The foot-and-a-half-long weapon was the blade of a military sabre, true enough, and Ryder had carried it from Carolina to Mississippi and back while wearing a Confederate uniform. But now it was a mere piece of its former self. Afoot among piled corpses in a north-Georgia pasture, he'd been covering his command's retreat. Battling a swarm of Yankees shifted to battling a single giant blue-clad footsoldier, probably the strongest adversary Ryder had ever had to tangle with . . .

"Oh!" Jess Kennesaw squealed. "I see what happened. The blade got broke off. And you must've ground it down on a stone, sharpened it into a cross between a short sword and a Bowie knife! How'd it happen?"

She seemed truly interested and Ryder didn't mind conversation. "There was hand-to-hand combat in the war once. A feller—a big feller— went 'round and 'round with me. He finally lost."

19

"You killed him with your busted sword?"

"No, his own weapon. But I fancied my old sabre, sharpened it just like you said, and kept it with me ever since. It's come in handy more than a few times."

She nodded solemnly. "I bet." Putting the sheathed sabre, the belt and the holstered Smith & Wesson beside her on the bale, she said abruptly, "Why'd you really come here?"

"Just passing through."

"You know, I believe you."

Ryder tried a smile. "That being the case, why don't you just take that old sawed-off sabre of mine and cut these ropes? I'd be obliged."

Fear edged her features. "Oh, I couldn't. Liz would skin me alive. She's real suspicious. Has got her a right to be, I reckon. Her husband, Joe, was shot in the back by a feller come here asking for a job. Most of our punchers had up and quit, thanks to Robeson's threatening talk in Yorktown. And sure enough, about a month after Joe's killer got away, our man, Lemuel, seen the bastard in town with Robeson."

"Yeah, looks bad for the rancher," Ryder said, wondering if he could get more information from Jess Kennesaw. Now, this Lemuel . . .

"Oh, you're wondering who Lemuel is? He's the very last puncher left here at the Rocking K. He's pretty old, but he's pretty tough, too. All us girls put a lot of stock in him, and that's why Liz wants him to help decide what ought to be done about you, Ryder." She glanced out the open door and studied the sun's angle. "Cathy should be back here with Lemuel in a couple hours. And the way Liz talked, she aims to stay over at the house for a spell." A long pause ensued. "You getting bored just lying there on the barn floor, Ryder? All tied up that way?"

"Well, as a matter of fact, I can think of about a hundred things I'd rather be doing about now." The friendly grin reappeared on his face. "Some of them with you, Jessica."

A wide smile was lighting her face too, and the aquamarine eyes had developed a strange glow. "Bet I know what you're going to suggest next, Ryder. That we put in the idle minutes having a good time together. And so's to get the most out of the romp, you really should be untied."

"Something like that."

The round little chin tilted up haughtily, and at the same time a sweetly smug expression came over Jessica Kennesaw's fine features. "I don't happen to believe that you work for Richard Robeson. But, you see, that's only a hunch. My sister-in-law, Liz, has got the right idea that we keep you from doing any harm till we find out more. There's simply too much at stake here at the Rocking K. So—" She swung her trim legs under her and stood up, the mocking smile still curling her mouth. "So, since I *do* find you attractive as hell and can't keep my hands off you—" She bent and stroked his cheek. "Or my lips either—" Suddenly she was on all fours and planting a hot kiss on his mouth, nearly smothering him. After a long moment she broke off. "I reckon I got me a problem. That is, unless—"

Ryder, gazing at the top of a head of flowing, shiny hair as black as a raven's wing, felt swift fingers at his waist undoing buttons. Then his pants popped open and a soft hand combed downward through the hair bush there to explore, find, and clasp.

"Oh, my!" she breathed.

"You do see why I got to do it this way, don't you Ryder? I mean, if you were to get the drop—"

As her fingers continued to work, Ryder gnawed his lip. "Oh, sure. I understand fine."

"No need to strain the way you are, trying to test those ropes. You can't get loose. Thank the Lord, though, Liz saw fit to stretch you on your back. Here, let me get those drawers of yours out of the way." She pulled down, and immediately fresh air bathed him from navel to knees. Already rail-spike hard, his length of gristle sprang mightily to attention.

"My God, you're huge, Ryder! I'm beginning to have second thoughts!"

"Well, untied I'd likely be better able to—"

"I'll manage!" And her hand was at the neckline of her dress, flipping buttons open until the garment hung open from top to hem.

She wore nothing underneath.

Now her eyes held a swimming mixture of emotions, the hot rage of desire warring with the awe she obviously held for Ryder's endowment, now fully engorged, throbbing and primed for action. And perhaps behind her hesitation lay an added bit of fear—fear that sister-in-law Liz might for some reason return to the barn.

22

"Aw, what the hell!" she crooned.

Now naked, her every magnificent curve seeming to glow in the soft light from the doorway, Jessica straddled Ryder in a single smooth motion and began to lower herself. When his drop-dewed tip was moistly cased between her thighs she paused, emitting a groan and fell forward so that a dollar-sized brown nipple hung a fraction of an inch from Ryder's mouth. He thrust his tongue out, met the warm, rubber nub of flesh and lapped it hungrily. Bullet hard in an instant, it tasted of lavender soap blended with salt sweat.

"Ah!" she groaned deeply.

She lunged her lower body down, impaling herself.

Ryder's massive member slid in smoothly and bottomed, wringing from the woman a long, extended sigh of gratification as she began to bounce wildly up and down. The big man could barely move in the bonds that held and chafed him; still the powerful surges of pleasure in his engulfed organ set him groaning along with the woman. She was totally in control, an unusual feeling for Ryder, but far from an unpleasant one.

Jessica Kennesaw increased her tempo of movement, then slacked it, holding the man under her at the brink without toppling him over. Suddenly she started to buck hard, and Ryder responded with upward thrusts of his own, meeting hers with sweat-moist slaps. "Ryder!" she whooped, as a strong trembling took her. Ryder felt her thighs tighten and the cushiony breasts pressed against his chest.

"So good! So good!' she moaned, and the ultimate shudder deep in her hot cave triggered Ryder, bringing too-long restrained juices up and out of him in a rush of sensation. A series of weak spasms capped the frenzy and the woman was quiet at last but for her rapid, shallow breaths. And then abruptly she came to life, and lifted a leg high to dismount.

She shook her head from side to side, waving the fall of long dark hair like a flag of victory. Scooping her dress up, she slipped it on, buttoning the fabric across the outthrust, perky breasts. "There. I do thank you, sir. I needed that." She moved to seat herself on the bale where his weapons lay, but happened to glance down at him. "Oh. I nearly forgot."

Dropping to squat, she swiftly stuffed Ryder back into his pants. It was a matter-of-fact movement, but the man read her to be as satisfied as the proverbial cat that got the cream. The blue-green eyes were dreamy, her face flushed.

"Hide the evidence," she giggled. "Say, you've got a while yet before the others are due back. You want some shut-eye, go ahead, take it."

Ryder, in his milked-dry state, felt his anvil-heavy lids already sinking. He was asleep in no time flat.

When the world exploded in gunfire, he was the most surprised man in it.

CHAPTER 3

How long he'd lain drowsing Ryder didn't know, but one thing was certain. Tied spread-eagled between stanchions on the floor of a deserted barn was no condition to be in with Colts and Winchesters booming and popping outside like doomsday thunder. A gang on horseback had to be bearing down on the ranch; hoofbeats mingled in the general din. The big man twisted his body, but only succeeded in bringing sharp pain to his chafed, raw wrists. Since the fracas outside had begun, five or six bullet holes had appeared in the wall above him, and in raids on ranches it was often only a matter of time till attempts were made to burn the buildings.

Damned tough ropes! And where the hell was Jessica?

As if in answer to Ryder's question, a shot rang out from the hayloft overhead. He recognized the report: it belonged to his own Smith & Wesson. Then a squeal of pain followed, and shuffling of feet over to and coming down the board ladder hung on the wall. "Oh, Ryder! Ryder!"

It was Jessica. She'd jammed his six-gun in her dress pocket while descending to the barn's main floor. Now she drew it forth and made for the door. As she ran past Ryder he spotted the bullet crease on the back of her clenched left hand.

"Jessica! Take the sabre and cut me free! Hurry!"

"Can't. You could be with *them!*" She was peering gingerly around the door jamb.

"With who?"

"Robeson's outfit, who else?"

She'd been noticed. A hail of hot lead poured through the doorway, whining and whistling in dangerous ricochet. The woman made haste to jump back out of view, and now was crouching beside Ryder.

"Damn it, I told you I'm not a Robeson man! If I was, would I have . . . Well, you know!"

"Ha! I done the lovemaking this morning, mister, though I am glad you furnished half the tools." She started to giggle, but winced instead.

"You're hurt! I don't want you hurt any more. What's going on out there?"

"Some of Robeson's riders. . ." Jessica Kennesaw edged toward the door again, her bleeding hand leaving a smeared red trail in the strewn hay. She stretched to look. "Oh, Jesus!"

A new flurry of hoofbeats was approaching. "What?"

"It's Cathy, trying to ride on in! But they're cutting her off!"

"Jessica, cut me loose!"

"They're riding down on her! They almost—"

26

"Jessica! Now!"

The woman whirled from the opening, a look of panic stretching the pretty features. The black hair hung dishevelled over shoulders trembling with indecision. "Don't let all of us be killed," Ryder said calmly.

Tears streaming down her cheeks, Jessica snatched up Ryder's sabre, sheath and all. Then with a sweep, she freed the wicked blade. "Do it!" Ryder commanded.

She obeyed, slashing the bonds holding his wrists, then freeing both feet. Ryder stumbled as he powered up, and had to catch himself against a stall wall, yet he made it to where his saddle lay in two strides. "Winchester . . . boot" he growled. Back at the doorway he levered a round into the chamber, threw the rifle to his shoulder and triggered.

Fifty yards across the flat that was the ranch yard, a rider on a galloping gray threw up his arms and pitched back over the horse's rump. Cathy Kennesaw wheeled Rambunction in a tight turn, raked heaving flanks with spurs and made for the barn. Three hardcase types were close behind.

A rifle inside the house barked. One rider went down in a pile up of thrashing horseflesh. The animal was shot in the neck, and huge gouts of blood gushed over hardcase and ground. When the man scrambled up, hotfooting for all he was worth toward the creek bank and a stand of willows, Liz fired again. Shirt front blossoming red, the fellow pitched head-first into the water and was still.

"Liz likes to do that," Jessica yelled in Ryder's

27

ear. "She's getting even for the killing of her Joe. Look—"

Ryder saw it too. Cathy was galloping past the corral very near to safety now, but two horsemen were bent on prevention. Ryder fired, jacked the weapon and prepared to fire again. The lead hardcase's face exploded in a crimson smear, his mount veered as he toppled. The plaid-shirted man, now Cathy's lone immediate threat, actually rode into her, horse colliding with horse and rebounding, all at a dead run. And the hard-riding bastard was now encircling the blond with an arm, hoisting her from the saddle! Once he had her, he reined in a circle, using Cathy as a human shield.

"Shit!" Ryder handed his rifle to Jessica and darted outside, the old thrill of combat rising in him as it had so often in the War. Bullets spanged in the dust as he crossed the yard, the men besieging the barn opening fire as this crew rode in for a kill. But before Cathy's captor could rein and spur, Ryder was at his stirrup, powerful hands locking on the man's belt, dragging him and Cathy from the saddle.

"Let the gal go!"

"Screw you!"

Ryder's arm drew back, roundhoused forward again to slam a fist solid as a chunk of granite to his adversary's jaw. The fellow's grip on the woman relaxed and she twisted away. From the corner of an eye Ryder saw her bolt for the barn. At the same time he waded in to attack the hardcase's midsection.

One, two, three solidly placed punches to gut

and chest flung plaid-shirt back into the solid poles of the corral. Caroming off, he tried to clinch with Ryder and also draw a long-barreled Remington Navy model. But the fellow was groggy. Ryder grabbed his shirt front and spun him around.

Hot lead intended for Ryder tore into the hardcase, who went limp. The big man flung him aside. Clawing the gun from the corpse's hand, Ryder cocked, crouched and shot in a single fluid motion. The bearded giant of a man riding down on him atop a mustang flung both hands high, emitted a shriek, fell.

Liz, aiming from the veranda, tagged the giant's sidekick, blowing him from his horse with a snap rifle shot. But the little fellow with the weasel face didn't die until, stirrup-dragged and screaming, his head was crushed by a flying hoof.

Cathy, at the barn, fired and winged a rider. He wheeled and galloped for the ridge.

Jessica eared back the hammer of Ryder's Smith & Wesson and let it drop. The slug plowed a man's arm, and he spurred for town.

Suddenly heavy silence ruled the Rocking K ranch. Ryder stood over the corpse by the corral and watched through clouds of drifting dust as the women, one by one, emerged from concealment. Cathy and Jessica came out of the barn, the raven-haired beauty's hand swathed in a crude bandage. Liz rose from behind the veranda railing, an old Winchester in hand, and strolled leisurely down the steps. When she reached ground level she waved at Ryder, and he saw her smile. She seemed positively jaunty at the extent of slaughter: no less than five riddled bodies littered the ranch yard.

These women's fears were not imaginary. Somebody meant business when a man was willing to pay other men to throw lead.

"Thanks, Ryder." The words were Cathy's as she came up to the big man. "You saved me, that's for sure, either from being kidnapped or killed. Those bastards killed Lemuel."

"What!" Liz stalked up to her blond sister-in-law's side, trailed by Jessica. "Did you say Lemuel is dead?"

"Dead as a horseshoe nail! I found him down by the line shack, told him about the stranger riding in," she said, indicating Ryder, "and how you'd ordered him knocked out and tied. Lemuel allowed he'd best ride back with me. Could be he'd recognize the feller. Well, when we got within a mile of the creek all hell broke loose. A bushwhacker took out Lemuel with a sneak shot from a ridge. Then at least a half dozen more hombres on horseback rode up and over and did their best to chase me down. Or, I should say, half of the outfit tried. The rest must've come on ahead to attack here before I could warn you. Well, I reckon it proves—"

"That Ryder, here, couldn't be any low-down shootist hired by Robeson," Liz said, completing Cathy's statement. "To risk his life the way he did for us—" Her face darkened. "Say, wait a minute. I recollect leaving you trussed tighter than a calf, mister." The blue eyes swung to Jessica.

Ryder stepped half in front of the black-haired woman, whose downcast expression made her look ready to make inconvenient admissions. "Lady, when the shooting started I was tied up in the barn, just like you left me. Only after Jessica got bullet-creased could I convince her to cut the ropes, let me help fight off this crew."

"Why, girl, you *are* hurt! Let me see!" She loosed the bandage, tightened her mouth at what she saw beneath. "Only a scratch, thank God, but we'll clean it up at the house. Jess, is what the man said true?"

"Yes, Liz."

"Oh, all right, girl. You did right, this time." The triumphant smile had returned. "We'd surely not have done this much damage to the bastards without Ryder." She thrust her hand at him to shake.

He took the hand. It was cool and firm. "Ma'am."

"Call me Liz."

"Liz, I'm happy to have helped."

The woman's look turned thoughtful. "Maybe you can be of more help. All our punchers are gone now. Lemuel was the last. If you'll stay to dinner, I may have a proposition."

Ryder responded with a nod. He hadn't eaten more than cracked corn and jerky since last night and his stomach was letting him know it.

"You're willing to listen, Ryder? Good," Liz said. Then she turned to the other women. "Cathy, see if you can round up the dead rascals' mounts, will you? We'll tie the bodies over the saddles, let the animals wander home." And to Jessica: "Now come with me. We'll tend that hand."

31

Ryder said, "Anything I can do?"

"Thanks for the offer. Find a spade in the tool shed. We'll take the buckboard out after we eat, fetch back Lemuel for burying."

"Somebody's going to throw a fit when those horses walk in carrying dead men."

She agreed. "And that'll be Robeson, back at his Slash-Diamond-Slash spread. Well, what's done is done, and he can't be made any more determined to run us off than he was already. Any more questions, Ryder?"

It was his turn to grin. "Reckon I do, at that."

"Well?"

"About that dinner? What you got cooking?"

Steak, potatoes and boiled turnips filled Ryder's plate, and he pitched in to the delicious fare with gusto.

Jessica, shy all of a sudden, tended to only her own food, leaving Cathy to watch with awe as the big man stowed his second helping.

At the head of the large kitchen table Liz ate daintily, hardly speaking. She sensed it was first things first with Ryder, and after gunplay came eats, a good country mile ahead of propositions involving danger. She studied him through lowered lashes. Rugged. Handsome. And he could handle himself, he'd made that plain enough out in the yard this morning.

"Coffee, Ryder?"

"Mm, how's that, Liz?" He talked as he chewed biscuit, and the words came out slurred.

"I said, would you care for more coffee?"

"You bet!"

Liz Kennesaw rose and crossed to the stove, bringing back the steaming pot. She sloshed dark brew into the mug beside the man's right hand and didn't spill a drop. When he'd emptied his plate he backed his chair away from the table and looked across at her inquiringly. "You got something to say to me?"

"Grub first, talk afterward," Liz proclaimed. "that's the way it's always been around here, even when our husbands were alive."

"Makes sense. I'm finished for now, though, and I reckon you've been for a little while, the other gals too." His glance scanned them, returned to the boss lady. "First, do you mind filling me in on what's been going on here? You said some things when you talked before, and so did Jessica, but I still don't have it all."

"You want it all?"

"Right." He swigged some coffee as he eyed her.

"Well all right, here goes." She exchanged looks with her two sisters-in-law, saw them nod. When she launched forth, the words came matter-of-factly at first, as if she were very weary. "Our husbands were three brothers, as I guess you must have gathered already. Joe, my man, Cathy's Jack, and Jessica's Jamie. Last name Kennesaw—the Rocking K brand. The Kennesaw boys started up here four years ago, after the War, married us girls one by one as the ranch took hold and the herd built. We all lived here together in this house, ran a few horses. But the main thing was cattle, good old Texas longhorns." A bemused smile played at the woman's lips. "Those were happy days."

"They didn't last?" Ryder demanded.

"They didn't last. About the same time the Kennesaw boys saw their venture start to pay off, Richard Robeson, a rich transplanted Kansan, made his own first bid to become top rancher in these parts. The first sections of his Slash-Diamond-Slash spread took in fresh-water springs, two of them. Water is the important thing here in the Texas panhandle. Without it grassland is about worthless."

Cathy nodded solemnly and Jessica joined in. The two young women seemed to be enjoying the yarn. Both sat hunched at the table over their coffee, chins in palms.

"So there was rivalry," Liz continued. "I guess there's bound to be whenever ranches butt up against each other. Robeson began expanding, buying out the various small landowners whose property bordered his. Soon he wound up with extensive territory, but not all connected and some without good water. Now, the great thing about the Rocking K is the creek you crossed getting here, Ryder. Robeson wants control of that water."

Ryder frowned. He could guess what was coming.

Liz traced a pattern on the tabletop with her finger. "About nine months back, Richard Robeson made an offer for the Rocking K. Caught my husband, Joe, one day in town, bought him a drink and announced he was determined to have this spread. That was the wrong approach. The Kennesaw boys were stubborn, and since they liked the country hereabouts, had worked hard to build this place up, they allowed they'd stay. Soon after that the trouble started."

"What kind of trouble?"

"Harassment. At first there were small incidents, our cowhands set on in Yorktown saloons and beaten. That happened to Tom Clark and Cal Weatherby. Then there'd be threats, and two or three punchers got scared and quit. Later still, it got so we'd find cattle shot out on the range."

Ryder's fingers fished a lucifer from his vest pocket. "Your husbands' killings. How'd those happen?"

"I told you some hands quit? Well, one day a man showed up here asking for a job. Joe talked to him out on the porch for a spell, then the pair of them wandered down to the corral. I was here in the kitchen baking bread when I heard the shot. All three of us womenfolk ran outside, just as the stranger was hightailing. Joe's body was behind the barn, face down in horse dung. He'd been gunned in the back."

The match Ryder held broke with a snap. "Damn! No wonder you women get spooked by drifters!"

"As for Jack and Jamie," Liz pressed on, "about a month went by after Joe's burying, and the boys were rounding up some cattle for sale. Lemuel found Cathy's husband crumpled in a gully, Jessica's man about a mile away on the open flat. Both dead, of course, but at least there'd been a fight. Both Kennesaws' Colts had been fired until empty, and the cattle they'd had with them were driven off."

"Rustlers?"

"That's what we were supposed to think."

"You got doubts?"

"Wouldn't you have?"

Ryder leaned back in his chair with a snort. Coming on the heels of Joe Kennesaw's murder, the younger brothers' deaths really did sound rotten as hell. "What does the sheriff think?"

"Bat Claymore? The old fart just sits at his desk over at the Yorktown jailhouse and tells all comers that, sure, Jack and Jamie Kennesaw were done in by cow thieves. Where'd the missing steers disappear to otherwise? And as for brother Joe, it must've been some passing-through owlhoot on the dodge that did him in. One now gone past catching, naturally." Liz Kennesaw laughed a bitter laugh. "As for any possibility Richard Robeson had to do with the killings—Claymore claims to know better. A fine, upstanding citizen of the county is Mr. Honest-Injun Robeson!"

When she'd finished, Ryder sat without speaking for a long time. Then, "And how long ago was all this?"

"Our husbands have been dead over six months."

"Must've been rough, holding on to the Rocking K, just you three women to boss the punchers. But, wait. You said there was only the one puncher, Lemuel?"

Liz said, "Robeson hired a few of our boys away, and some others left after being threatened. Two quit, claiming they couldn't abide boss-ladies in pants. That left one lover boy, hot to bed me, Cathy and Jess. *We* let *him* go! And if it's been rough, running the spread ourselves, there was no choice."

"We simply couldn't sell out to Robeson," Cathy put in. "Not after he had our menfolk killed." Her voice was bitter. "And, you know, once Jack, Jamie and Joe were in the ground, Robeson's cash-offer price dropped by half."

"Which we think *proves* that Robeson was behind our trouble," Jessica added.

"Right." Liz combed fingers through her long red hair, then dropped hands in frustration to the tabletop. "But we've got a plan. Round up our herds and stage a drive. With fair Abilene market prices, we could clear enough to bring men in from out of town, maybe a gunslinger or two to fight a range war. Or at least hold Robeson off till we can find another buyer."

Ryder drummed the tabletop with restless fingers. "Robeson. Sounds like a mean bastard. Wife could be giving him hell, I suppose."

Liz snorted.

"Man's got no wife," Jessica put in. "No women at all at the Slash-Diamond-Slash."

He got up abruptly. "Let me think on this whole business a spell."

And with the three women's eyes following him, Ryder strolled outside.

CHAPTER 4

He spurred a full-chested and fast sorrel from the Rocking K remuda along the road to Yorktown, and as the treeless rangeland flowed past, thought hard over the day's happenings. After dinner Liz Kennesaw had tracked him down under a creekside cottonwood and talked proposition. Ryder figured the thirty-a-month-and-found wages she offered were acceptable, but he would sure as hell insist on doing more than a typical puncher. Like protect the three young widows from further mayhem.

And it wasn't merely that he'd signed on; there was a fact he couldn't get off his mind. Here was where he'd have brought Holly if she'd lived. And if he'd been killed, Holly would've been the one trying to make the ranch a success without him. He'd want someone to help her, wouldn't he?

Liz, Cathy and Jessica blamed their neighbor, Robeson for the ambush slaying of Lemuel and the raid on the ranch—and who else stood to profit from such carryings on?

Ryder proposed going into town alone. The last

spate of killings had to be reported to the law, and by doing it he'd accomplish dual goals: meet the sheriff, plus serve notice that the Kennesaw women had a new protector. One a heap less easy-going and slow than poor old Lemuel.

And once that item of information started circulating in Yorktown and the territory around about, he'd likely draw trouble like a cow pie draws flies. Well, good. Let the rats in the woodpile have a try. One sure way—and the fastest—to pull rats from cover was with strong bait. He'd been bait before, it was no big deal. All you had to do was be an extra bit wary when the shit started to fly.

Which was what he'd assured Liz once she'd finished saying a few words over Lemuel's fresh grave. So she'd given her go-ahead, backed by Cathy and, he supposed, Jessica. Funny thing about Jess, the black-haired beauty hadn't been saying much, was nowhere near as uninhibited as she'd shown herself when making love. Maybe she feared his telling on her. Still, her quietness around him and those downcast eyes had their effect. Ryder hours ago had ceased considering any immediate follow-up to their little frolic in the barn.

"Yo, fella." He drew rein on the sorrel, let him stand in the road and blow. Far ahead the buildings of a town squatted, small under the vast spread of blue sky, but a considerable place by local standards. The Kennesaw women had described it: a jailhouse, livery stable, cafe, bank, hotel, two mercantiles, a half-dozen saloons. No church or school. Just the things really necessary this deep in cattle country.

A half-hour later he rode in.

A couple of the saloons looked prosperous, being big enough to offer gambling and, no doubt, strings of barmaid-whores. Ryder trotted by, looking for the jail. He found it holding down a streetcorner next to the Sunflower, a seedy hotel with a cheerful name. Dismounting at the hitchrail in front, Ryder sized the street: a usual amount of ranch-wagon and horseback traffic for a late afternoon. He expected things would liven up later when ranch hands on the town would overflow the drinking establishments and disperse Yorktown's appearance of drowsiness.

The door under the sign reading "Sheriff" was shut despite the sweatbox Texas heat. Ryder turned the knob and walked in.

An L-shaped room lit and cooled by a single window contained a desk, a couple of scuffed and scarred ladderback chairs and a weapon cabinet complete with the biggest padlock Ryder had ever seen. Behind the desk, positioned at the room's dogleg to afford an easy scan of the cell area to the rear, a man sat shuffling wanted dodgers. A round fortyish face, canonball belly, and pinned-on tin star fit Liz Kennesaw's description of Bat Claymore. "Sheriff?"

The lawman's jowls shook as he looked up. Piglike eyes, even to a pinkish cast. "That's me." He didn't seem happy to be disturbed by anything that could smack of duty. The flabby lips hung open in a sneer.

"My name's Ryder," the big man told him.

"Hired on just today at the Kennesaw's Rocking K." Ryder caught the fleeting glitter in the lawman's eyes before they returned to dullness. "There's been gunplay out at the ranch, sheriff. This morning seven hardcases rode in shooting, five caught lead and sort of hung around. One Rocking K puncher was killed, a Lemuel Sorenson. Know him?"

"I seen the old feller around. You say there was a raid? Who of t'other side got killed?"

Ryder pulled up a chair and sat down. "Didn't know them, don't know where they came from. But if they were sent, their bossman is going to find out what happened. Me and the women tied them to their horses, shooed the cayuses off to wander back wherever they came from."

Bat Claymore's bootsoles hit the floor and he rose. "Christ. The Rocking K want more trouble? Any pals of the dead'uns could be back there by now." The tiny eyes grew sly. "You say the Kennesaw females are out there alone?"

"I didn't say alone. And anybody going after them will have his hands full. That house is like a fort." Ryder lied easily. Although he doubted at this time that the lawman was directly involved against the Rocking K, acknowledging any ranch weakness to a townsman made no sense. Instead he proceeded to the next stage of his visit. "Claymore, I wonder what you're going to do about this morning's fracas."

"What the hell is there to do? Unless any of the attacking sidewinders can be identified as hands from Slash-Diamond—" He stopped, realizing

42

suddenly he said too much.

Ryder grinned lopsidedly. "Did anybody say they reckoned Richard Robeson was mixed up in this?"

"I just thought—I mean, everybody in these parts has been following the sort of feud that's been shaping up between them Kennesaw women and Mr. Robeson. Naturally—"

Ryder waved aside more bullshit, and Claymore's voice wound down gradually to embarrassed silence. "It *is* natural enough, what you were saying, sheriff," Ryder said. "By now everybody in north Texas knows Cathy, Liz and Jessica's suspicions about their land-grabbing neighbor. Now, you aren't going to do much denying that the man has already gobbled up most of the land in the county, are you?" Ryder was enjoying Bat Claymore's fist-clenching, mouth-twisting frustration. The big man made himself more comfortable by crossing his legs.

"Can't nobody deny Mr. Robeson's bought up some ranches—"

"I hear you done the investigating when the Kennesaw brothers got gunned down. Found nothing, it appears, you could make an arrest on?" He fingered a lucifer match from his vest pocket and thrust it between his teeth.

"Course not. Drifters done them killings: the longhorns run off weren't never seen again. If I could've caught the rustlers I'd have jailed 'em, but they'd cleared out."

"Convenient."

The piggy eyes narrowed in puzzlement. "What

43

did you say?"

"Oh, never mind." Tilting the black flat-brim back on his head, Ryder came to the point. "Sheriff, what happened six months ago is important, but I came in here expecting nothing but excuses. What I didn't expect was you not seeming to give a shit about today's shootings. You aim to do anything to trace Lemuel's killers?"

"Shit, if you and the Kennesaws killed five raiders, justice is likely done."

"Like I said, two got away."

"You didn't try to track 'em?"

"Job for a posse. You might track the horses we sent home with the corpses too."

"Well-ll. . ." Sheriff Bat Claymore scratched his ribs with broken-nailed fingers. "Horses with corpses, pretty undependable. If the animals was stolen, they'd home someplace innocent, wrongly involve some good people."

Ryder said, "Stolen horses?"

"Yeah, and good people blamed for something they never done. Why Mr. Robeson—"

"Who said anything about Robeson?"

"You did, a minute ago. Hell, Ryder, any damn fool can see what you're about. That redhead Kennesaw woman blames Mr. Robeson for the Rocking K's troubles. She's been in this office plenty, believe me. Now she's roped you in, a pretty smart feller, only a mite too easy bamboozled by sweet talk. Now you're runnin' her errands."

Ryder took the match from his mouth and snapped it, letting the pieces fall to the floor. He got up slowly, keeping his flint-gray eyes fixed on the bloodshot ones of Claymore. "Hold on. I was there this morning when those riders came in whooping and shooting. Defending myself and those women had nothing to do with being bamboozled—it was plain staying alive. And I helped bury the puncher Lemuel, who I hear was a damn good man. But it looks like nothing I say now is going to set you to trying to find out who sent those hardcases."

"Can't be proved they was sent," Claymore opined. "Could've acted all on their own."

"Shit! Well, good day to you, sheriff. I'll be moseying. No sense wasting more time."

"Obliged. I *am* a busy man."

Ryder paused going through the door. "I don't much care about *your* time, sheriff," he grinned, snapping his hatbrim. "It's *my* time I happen to be thinking of."

The Elephant Saloon's high false front bore a large-scale representation of the animal. Ryder squinted up at the faded, peeling colors and tried to decide: this place or the similar-sized Palace across the street? It wasn't only a question of cold beers; the main motive for the big man remained gaining information. His mind was made up when a horseman galloping in the street wheeled tightly, swung down and dropped his reins over the hitch-rail Ryder stood beside. The newcomer strode to and shouldered through the Elephant's bright green batwings.

The horse bore the Slash-Diamond-Slash brand.

45

Ryder walked inside in the man's wake.

It was one of the premier saloons, he saw at a glance. The massive bar of inlaid mahogany was backed not only with mirrors and shelving for bottles, but genuine art. A painting of a life-size female nude was the central rendering, but there were other pictures as well: a rampaging grizzly bear, a magnificent eight-point bull elk, a hissing and spitting puma. Ryder bellied up under the puma to wait for the barman, who was busy elsewhere. The neckless giant in the stained white apron was rousting a swamper. The words, "Worthless son of a bitch . . . lollygagging loafer" drifted on the smoky air.

Although only a few drinkers lined the bar, the man who'd used the Slash-Diamond-Slash cayuse had gone straight to a table, Ryder noted, and now was talking animatedly to a trio of denizens. All were rough puncher types save for one, an almost-kid got up gaudily in frock coat, gaberdines, ruffled shirt. The outfit of a tinhorn. The young man's pasty-white, delicate hands idly toyed with a deck of cards.

"What'll you have, mister?"

Ryder looked around and into the beefy face of the barkeep. "Your beer cold?"

The man shrugged.

"I'll take one anyway." Ryder tossed a nickel on the bar and watched it disappear.

Sipping thirstily at his frothing tumbler, the big man was aware of being scrutinized. The barman hadn't moved off, but merely positioned himself, leaning, against the backbar. Of course, there was

46

no law requiring service and flight, but the fellow's obviousness irritated Ryder. "Something the matter?"

"Don't I know you from someplace?"

"I reckon not. Don't recollect ever laying eyes on you before today."

"Wait a minute. You had a beard. You ever wear a beard?"

"Maybe." Ryder's eyes narrowed. He'd worn a beard during the War, never before or since.

Suddenly the barkeep turned his back and was very busy handling glass-polishing chores down at the bar's remote far end. Behavior funny as hell. Unless the fellow had managed to recall where and under what circumstances he'd seen Ryder before. As to that time and place, the big man, despite hard consideration, remained absolutely in the dark.

The Slash-Diamond-Slash rider and his cohorts had stopped talking, and the young man in gambler's attire was in the process of dealing out a hand of solitaire. Everybody appeared settled down to wait.

Ryder was waiting, too, but for what he didn't quite know. He did know, however, that when the barkeep delivered a fresh whisky bottle to the crew at the table, soft-spoken words were exchanged, followed by glances his way that didn't look too friendly. So he nursed his beer, studied the animal pictures. It couldn't have been more than ten or fifteen minutes before all hell broke loose in the person of a new arrival.

Not a midget, exactly, but a little man—four-foot-ten or -eleven—burst through the batwings. He swept the ten-gallon hat from his head and shouted, "Slash-Diamond-Slash riders, over to the hotel, pronto! There's trouble! Big trouble!"

The quartet at the rear table were on their feet in an instant, kicking chairs against the walls in their haste, spilling glasses of whisky. "What? What's that, Shorty?"

"The hell you say!"

"Trouble? What kind?"

All but the dandied-up young fellow made for the door, spurs jangling, boots slipping in the sprinkled sawdust underfoot, oversetting spittoons. The little puncher, Shorty, was shouting, "It's the boss! Mr. Robeson! Somebody just tried to shoot him!"

"Christ! We better get a move on!"

"Outa m'goddamn way!"

All at once it was very quiet inside the Elephant. Several drinkers remaining at the bar stood with mouths open, simply staring. The young gambling man softly ruffled his deck. Robeson shot at? What could that mean? Ryder wondered. He slid his glass along the bartop, carefully adjusted the work gunbelt at his hip and prepared to stroll outside.

"Mister?"

"Yeah?" He was answering the swamper, who'd moved close and now stood nervously, fiddling with his broom handle.

"Your name's Ryder, ain't it?"

Ryder studied the man. Though not old, his face was lined, his body bent. Broken veins purpled his nose and reddened his eyes. "Ryder, that's me. How'd you know?"

The swamper nodded toward the rear table. "I was listenin'. I always listen all I can. Burl, the puncher you followed in, he called you Ryder."

"Yeah, well, listen, feller, I got to be—"

"You step outside, Ryder, you're gonna be sorry. Damn sorry."

Outside, the Slash-Diamond-Slash crew was mounting up. If he was going to tag along, he'd need to rush. "Sure, sure."

"You ain't goin', Mr. Ryder, you're stayin'. Listen to old Terry Shea."

And all at once, Ryder was all ears. The muzzle of Terry Shea's deadly little derringer was screwed deep in his floating ribs.

CHAPTER 5

"Don't get edgy, now, Mr. Ryder," Terry Shea said, "but, yeah, m'gun is loaded. You and me, we're gonna walk over to the back door. Just like we're heading outside to pee."

The little swamper prodded with the derringer, and Ryder clamped his jaw. The other patrons of the Elephant weren't paying attention; and even if they had been, couldn't be counted on in this fix. Shea could blow Ryder into eternity in a split second.

"Let's go," Shea breathed.

Probably the best place to try and turn the tables was along the way out back. Ryder moved slowly toward the door down by the bar end. Where in blue hell was the bartender? If he'd put in an appearance, he'd likely have strong words for a swamper not swamping. And any distraction, even a slight one, was all Ryder felt he needed.

"All right, Ryder, only a few steps more." They were opposite the solitary card-dealer now, but the young fellow didn't look up. "Now, walk on through and out, Ryder. And you better not try anything."

Shit! They were outside in an alley, and an alley gone nearly dark with the onset of night. As soon as they'd cleared the saloon steps, Shea had taken a step away to be out of reach. Unfortunately for Ryder, *he* remained in reach of a slug from Shea's gun.

"Now what?" Ryder wanted to know.

"I had to keep you from going after those Slash-Diamond-Slash hands."

"So?"

"So I done what I done." Terry Shea's face was an indistinct blur, but there was a catch in his voice. How to read the man?

"Shea, what I ever done to you, I can't guess, but—"

"They was settin' up a trap for you. I overheard 'em at the table. Burl—he was the one come in with word from Robeson—said that Shorty was on his way to draw the outfit outside with some lyin' nonsense. And when you followed, they were to gun you down."

Ryder's eyes went to slits. "I should believe this?"

"They said you rode for the Rocking K, so you're an enemy. Believe old Terry Shea or don't believe him, Mr. Ryder, but I told God's truth. Now I done it, I reckon there's no need for this." Ryder saw a wink of light on steel as the other man pocketed the derringer. "Thing's all busted anyway, don't really shoot. Hell, if the blame thing did work, I'd sell it in a minute, buy a bottle. That's old Terry Shea's way."

Ryder relaxed, let his hand drift from the Smith
& Wesson's walnut grip. He believed the swamper.
"Terry, you're a drinking man."

"Yep."

"Let me buy you a drink. I owe you."

He caught Shea's mouth corners turning faintly
up. "Reckon I'll pass. I got to work in the Elephant to eat. You ain't too popular around here,
Mr. Ryder."

If the swamper would talk, he was willing to
listen. "Terry, on account of why?" Ryder questioned. "You saved my life tonight, so you got
some sense of fair play. If I'm going to be able to
stay alive, don't you see I got to get a better idea of
where I stand, what I'm up against?"

Terry Shea nodded. "Awright. You're up against
a fat cat name of Richard Robeson, ranches the
Slash-Diamond-Slash. Biggest spread in these
parts. But it ain't big enough for Robeson. He's
plumb greedy, and it ain't the kid, neither. It's him.
Him."

"Kid?"

"He's got him a young son. Look, Mr. Ryder, I
got to be gettin' back inside. Any minute Gus, the
barkeep, could step out here a-huntin' me."

"Wait. I've heard tell of Robeson, how he's used
strong methods to force his buy-outs of ranchers
'round about. But have all the folks he's cheated
cleared out? Or are some of them hanging on in
Yorktown?"

Terry Shea edged through shadows toward the
saloon's back steps. "Oh, there's a few of them he
bought out as have stuck."

"I'd like to meet them. Would you pass the word? I believe Liz Kennesaw would like to meet them too."

"You're stayin' in town?"

"Not tonight, but I'll be back. See what you can do?"

The back door of the saloon burst open, spilling a bright rectangle of light across the alley. "Shea, goddamn you, are you out here? Let me find your lazy ass, I'll kick it!"

In the shadows close by the wall, Shea hissed, "I got to go."

"Will you pass the word like I asked?"

"Oh, awright!"

And the bent little man raced up the steps and through the door.

Ryder ambled up the alley toward the street. At the corner he slowed, halted, then eased out onto the boardwalk and threw a glance at the hitchrail in front of the Elephant. The sorrel was there, among a dozen or more other horses now, and looked reasonably content in their company. So what to do next? Terry Shea had warned him to beware, and he was inclined to take the warning seriously. So he'd figured to see Richard Robeson himself, if the rancher was in town. He had no way of knowing whether, as Shorty had stated, Robeson was at the hotel. Ryder had no way of knowing either if, having been at the hotel, Robeson had by now left for the Slash-Diamond-Slash—or elsewhere. Still, while in town, he wanted to accomplish as much as possible. A casual inquiry at the hotel couldn't do much harm. Not if he kept his eyes peeled for that bunch of bastards that had planned to spring the trap.

The Sunflower: a big two-story structure, false-fronted like most of the business places on Yorktown's main street. From all the lights burning in the upper windows Ryder figured there were a lot of guests. He saw himself standing down here in the dark street, watching till he spotted Robeson, then making his way inside and up to the rancher's room. . .

But unfortunately, he didn't know what the son-of-a-bitch looked like. Liz Kennesaw had had time to describe the sheriff to him while he was saddling up the sorrel, but he'd wanted to get started and . . .

No sense crying over spilt milk. He had another idea. Robeson's men obeyed orders, therefore all he had to do was ask for a palaver, let the old fellow call off his dogs, and the two of them could have a fruitful meeting in real comfort. He tugged his hatbrim low and strolled leisurely up onto the hotel's gingerbread-railed, chair-studded porch.

Only one person occupied a chair under the hung lanterns at the head of the steps. A middle-aged fellow, crag-faced and with hair the color of tin, sat rocking, rocking. The man wore a frock coat of black, gray flannel trousers, and an indigo cravat with silver stickpin. A book lay across the bony knees, and an emaciated finger marked a place in the pages.

Ryder nodded in passing, entered and strode up to the desk.

"Yessir?" was the bespectacled clerk's greeting.

"You got a guest by the name of Richard Robeson?"

"Well-ll . . ."

"No trouble. Just want to leave a message."

"He's here."

"Got something to write with?"

The writing equipment was shoved across. Ryder wrote clearly, as for an army requisition: "We should meet. I represent the Kennesaws and the Rocking K. No gunslicks. (Signed) A. Ryder." He folded the paper three times, handed it to the clerk.

"You want this delivered?"

"You bet."

The man peered at Ryder with pursed lips, walked around the counter and over to the door.

"Gone."

"Huh?"

"Mr. Robeson is gone. That was him sitting in the chair. You didn't know?"

Ryder scratched his head. "Never saw the feller before. No way I could've known him. Sure moves out quiet, don't he?"

The hotel clerk said nothing for a long moment. Then, "I can't say whether he'll be back. He's still registered, of course, but—"

Up the street came a commotion of riders, the Slash-Diamond-Slash contingent from the saloon, plus a dozen more. At their head spurred the gray-haired man. Richard Robeson galloped past looking neither left nor right.

"Never mind the note," Ryder told the clerk.

Time for Ryder to haul ass too.

When the sorrel splashed through the creek it was past midnight, and moonglow showed Ryder the Rocking K yard deserted—almost. At the corral gate he swung down, stripped saddle and bridle, and turned the tired animal in. Only then did he spin on his bootheel and plod leisurely toward the house. The closer he got, the less indistinct she appeared there, lounging where the dark shadow of the building fell across the steps. She'd changed from a dress to a thin nightrail, and he could just make out the pale circle that was her face.

When he stood over her and she still didn't speak, Ryder broke the silence. "Evening."

"Good evening." Jessica tossed her head and the long raven curls brushed his hand. "You're getting back late, Ryder."

"Too late, likely. How's your bullet crease?"

She waved her bandaged hand carelessly. "Aches. It's just a scratch, I know, but it's been keeping me awake. Pretty tired by now, though. Reckon I'll turn in."

"Good idea."

"You can tell Liz and Cathy and me in the morning what you learned in town."

"I'll tell you in the morning."

"I'm glad you're safe. The others said you'd be," she sighed. "Well, I'm turning in. We fixed up a cot for you in the bunkhouse, clean blanket and all. Sleep well."

"Jessica."

Where the side of him fell in shadow, she squeezed his hand. She shook her head slightly as well. So someone was watching. From one of the dark windows, up behind the black-haired beauty or else upstairs. Ryder got the message. "Well, reckon that bed is going to feel right good to these old bones. Good night, Jessica."

She stood up, and the high, pointed breasts strained the gown fabric. "See you in the morning."

As Ryder made his way to the bunkhouse, he glanced back once. A curtain at the upper-corner window dropped into place like a silent ghost.

The empty whisky bottle exploded in a shower of glass.

"Nice shot." Ryder pushed off the barn's unpainted wall and took a step across the yard toward Liz. She holstered her colt with a flourish, preparing for anther practice draw.

"I make a lot of nice shots, Ryder. Now watch that can set up over on that rock." She went into a crouch, slim hand hovering over the big .45 Colt's handle, then made her move. She wasn't fast. In fact her thumb caught the six-gun's hammer and the weapon was deflected coming out of the greased-leather sheath. But when she triggered, the fixed tin can grew a punched, round hole. "Damn."

"No need to knock yourself, Liz. You killed your can." He smiled easily.

"But if it could've shot back, I'd be the one sprouting holes, sure as hell. That's why I practice every morning before breakfast. With a range war. . ."

The day was already hot. Beads of sweat hung in Ryder's mustache and beaded up uncomfortably along the ridge of his brow. Still, he knew the woman would stand here in the sun until she was made to feel right about her chances in the battle she foresaw against Robeson. Clearly, success to her meant prowess with weapons, and she could be right.

Or, as another view held, all the gunplay she and her sisters-in-law were capable of mounting would still be fruitless in the face of numbers. How many men could Robeson throw against the Rocking K? Twenty? A couple dozen? In the end, tricks and strategy might tip the balance. Liz needed to start spreading her eggs around in a lot more baskets.

A triangle clamored up at the house, the signal that Jessica had hot side meat, gravy and biscuits on the table. Liz smiled back at Ryder as she thumbed a handful of shells from her gunbelt and proceeded to reload. "Well, that's all for now," she said. "Let's go get some grub. *And* that war council you promised now that you met Robeson."

"But I didn't meet him, remember? Just managed a quick look at the feller while he was getting ready to leave town."

"Whatever. We can—"

"Liz! Liz!" The shouts erupted from the throat of Cathy as the big blonde flung out of the house and toward them across the dust of the yard. "My God! My God!"

"What?"

"What?" Ryder echoed, swiveling his head as he started to run, scanning the distance for the cause of trouble.

Cathy pulled to a stop, gasping for breath. Her hair was disarrayed, shirt half buttoned over full, round breasts. "I was upstairs making beds. Glanced out the window, then I saw . . . it! Not dead men, of course that's worse, but—well, after driving them off yesterday I figured we had them licked, maybe. So w-when—"

Liz snapped, "Damn it, girl—"

"Hold it," Ryder interrupted, then touched the blonde's shoulder with a gentling hand. "It's all right, Cathy. Tell us what you saw."

"From up there you can see it, not down here. It must've happened in the night. Ryder, Liz! Dead cattle! Dozens scattered, all the way to the ridge!"

Liz froze, peering at Ryder by her side. Looking past the women, the big man saw them in the sky: swooping buzzards gathered for the feast. His teeth clenched.

"Dear God, when will it end?" Liz said.

"Not till Robeson learns a lesson. I'll hitch up the buckboard, gal. And Liz, here's what you got to wear . . ."

CHAPTER 6

Storm clouds piled in the west like thunder-gray mountains as the buckboard lurched toward Yorktown. Ryder wasn't ready to take on the Slash-Diamond-Slash outfit yet on their own ground, but he was ready to do battle.

"Oh," Liz Kennesaw said, gripping the buckboard seat as they topped a bump. "Dark at midmorning. Ryder, it hasn't rained in months. This could be a bad one."

"Could be the best thing for us if the weather gets bad. Keep Robeson and his boys to home while we make hay."

"In Yorktown? What's to do in that place but buy supplies?" She gnawed her lip. "Never should have left Cathy and Jess back at the ranch. And why in the world have me get all dressed up?" She fiddled with the pleats of her full, primrose-yellow silk skirt.

"As to the first, the gals will be fine. As to the second, you'll see when we get there—I hope!"

"Hope? You don't actually know, Ryder, what's gong to happen?"

His grin twisted and twitched his mustache. "I'm seeing a real woman, at least. Not a pants-wearing, pistol-toting she-cat."

The redhead lapsed into sullen silence. Several miles of jolting, rutted road passed under the buckboard's wheels and then: "Ryder," Liz said, "about yesterday and what you told the girls and me at breakfast. It's pretty clear Sheriff Claymore tipped Robeson you'd been nosing around. That's why the trap at the saloon Terry Shea warned you of. So why didn't Robeson grab the chance to go after you later? At the hotel, or on the way back to the Rocking K?"

Ryder shrugged. "What I went to the hotel for was to talk with the feller without anger, try and get him to agree to meet with us. Five of his men died in the raid. I aimed to tell him more were doomed unless he backed off. Make him realize the Rocking K can't be bought with bullets."

Dark skies were overhead now, and though rain didn't quite seem ready, lightning flickered and there was the low drumlike roll of distant thunder. Liz Kennesaw shouted above the rising wind. "You're a reasonable man, Ryder, but Robeson isn't. Life's cheap to him, and there are always more gunslicks for hire with money. What do you think about the slaughtered cattle?"

"Rough." He slapped the reins on the backs of the team to hurry them. "Kind of backs up your notion he'll stop at nothing. Funny, though."

"Yes?"

"Killing stock is like killing the ranch itself. Most cattlemen see this, even those willing to lose hands aplenty in a bloody range war. A reason I want more than ever to get face to face with this Robeson, look in his eyes. Know my enemy, what there is about him that makes him different."

"One thing. He's crazy."

Ryder swung to her, swivelling on the seat. "Is that true, or just talk?"

Ahead, Yorktown had come in view, the lowering clouds seeming to press the ugly excuses for buildings to earth. When Liz Kennesaw didn't answer his question, Ryder pressed. "Well? You've dealt with Robeson. If he's loco, that means a whole different plan. What do you say?"

Her voice was small. "I don't know for sure."

Raindrops spit from the sky. Ryder reached behind him, brought up a bundle. Grinning, he said, "Almost to town, but this is one time 'almost' ain't enough. Slickers. Pull 'em out."

She did.

They rolled into Yorktown in a downpour, but huddled dry under the sheets of oilcloth.

The clerk at the Sunflower Hotel said, "Yessir, I recollect you."

"We want a room."

"*A* room?" The bespectacled eyes gazed across the open registry book at Liz. She was blotting rainwater from her face with a hanky. "Afternoon, Mrs. Kennesaw."

"Good afternoon, Elmer. Mr. Ryder meant to say two rooms. Don't we need two rooms, Mr. Ryder?"

"For a few hours' meeting? I don't guess—"

63

"Two rooms, Elmer."

"Yes, ma'am!"

As they climbed the stairs Liz muttered, "I don't have much left in this godforsaken town, Ryder, but I do have my reputation. All us Kennesaw women are widows, and people are all too ready to make whores of us in their minds. Once that happens the decent sort turn their backs."

"You don't need to go on. My mistake, back there. Here're the rooms, side-by-side, two-oh-one and two-oh-four. Yeah, a key—" The flimsy, varnished pine panel swung inward as he touched the latch. "Overlooks the street. Not bad." Ryder tossed his sodden hat on the bed, took Liz's slicker and stripped out of his own.

"What now?"

"Like I said on the way here, I want us to meet with some of Robeson's other enemies. Folks whose ranches he bought up in the last few years and likely cheated. The way Terry Shea talked, some of them stayed on in Yorktown and can be got together on short notice. That's where I'm off to now, to locate Shea. Once I palaver with this bunch tonight I figure to know Robeson's weak spots. Maybe fellers will even want to throw in with us in our fight. We can hope."

"Eventually you'll confront Robeson?"

"Eventually. And when that time comes, I'll be prepared." He reached, laid a hand on her soft, bare arm. *"We'll* be prepared. You're in this too. That's why I wanted you along and looking fine like you do. It's another idea I had."

She peered at him sidelong. "Idea? What?"

"Remember, you described trouble? Menfolk not abiding boss-ladies who wear pants?"

Of course she did.

"Well, you're not wearing pants now. It's a hell of a lot easier, I say, catching flies with honey 'stead of vinegar!"

Ryder took the stairs down to the lobby two at a time and waved to the clerk only in passing as he made for the street. From the rain-slashed board-walk, shanking it toward the Elephant, Ryder glanced over his shoulder. Liz had lit a lamp. The window of her upper-corner room was a cheerful yellow rectangle glowing against the gloomy gray of the drab building. Then a gust of wind battered his face and eyes, and he dropped his head, rushed on.

The Elephant's long bar was deserted. You could never tell about these things. If a storm trapped drinkers in a place the whole crowd would likely stick, weather making the excuse for the killed time and lapped-up crackskull whisky. On the other hand, a storm could keep the boys away. Luck of the draw, and the barkeep did look extra unlucky and morose today.

"Beer," Ryder ordered as he shook himself dry like a spaniel.

"Right." A foaming mug was set before the big man.

No Terry Shea could be seen, but Ryder's hunch held that the swamper would show up soon. The minute he did, Ryder would put the bug in his ear to get the bought-out ranchers together. Meanwhile, the beer tasted delicious.

Now, if that barkeep would direct those droop-lidded, curious eyes of his elsewhere . . .

"Mister?"

"Yeah, the beer's fine."

The barkeep didn't take the hint, just hovered under the portrait of the angry grizzly, holding a wet glass and a towel in his big hands as if waiting. Finally, he slammed the glass down on the mahogany, flung the towel over his shoulder. The flushed, beefy face worked another minute and then the man blurted, "Hell, it ain't the beer that's on my mind. The thing that is—well, it's between you and me."

This was the fellow who yesterday had asked Ryder if he'd sometime worn a beard. There'd been no chance to prolong the discussion and it had dropped, but, plainly, something was troubling him. Ryder's eyes slitted, studying the man. No, he could swear the slack face and jutting chin weren't familiar, and his memory was usually faultless. The hand resting near the Smith & Wesson flexed warily, yet how often did real trouble announce itself this slowly?

"My name's Blake," the man announced. "That mean anything to you, mister?"

He could answer without hesitating. "Can't say as it does. Look, Blake, you still figure you know me from someplace?"

"I done figured it out already. You're Lieutenant Ryder, of General Stonewall Jackson's cavalry back in the War. Oh, don't puzzle to recognize me, though. We never met, not face to face. It was my wife you knew in Virginia."

Christ! An outraged husband? But back then he'd been head over heels in love with Holly, had only taken an available woman on rare occasions when his need had been overwhelming, the pressures of war unendurable. But never a married woman.

Now Blake the bartender was smiling at him. "Sarah Blake. You *must* remember. How many babies did you deliver back in them years? Haw!"

It came back to Ryder in a rush. The backwoods cabin on the hardscrabble, rocky farm, far from any main road. A rainy night had turned the trails to bog. Separated from his regiment, horse near foundering, he'd been riding in a well-nigh exhausted state himself when he heard the screams. There hadn't even been a lamp in the cabin, just candles, candles and the woman on the rumpled pallet, far gone in labor. He'd boiled water on the crude hearth, done what he could. Eventually the baby came: female and tiny, squalling and kicking. A healthy child. And Sarah Blake was a healthy woman, although temporarily in bad shape when he found her. He'd left mother and babe at dawn and ridden out. One summer day in 1863.

"Haw! You *do* remember!"

"I remember." She'd been a pretty woman, and had stayed that way through her whole ordeal. But there'd still been fear in her eyes, and justifiably so. Of course Ryder had known there was someone else in the cabin. The Yankee uniform blouse wasn't well hidden, and he'd discovered it in his search for rags. The uniform of a wounded private.

67

It was covered with blood.

Ryder had figured Sarah to be enmeshed in enough troubles without his capturing her man as well. Leaving her totally alone with the baby and without hope. Especially since the man had to have deserted, likely panicked at his wife's condition. Let the poor, pathetic family be, he'd decided.

Now the man stood before him. And apparently he wanted to express gratitude. Ryder returned his smile. "How is Sarah? And little—"

"Jenny. We called the gal-child Jenny. Both of 'em are fine. We got a house here in town, and they're home in it right now. And Lieutenant Ryder?"

"Uh huh?"

"Thanks. You coulda took me easy that day. I didn't have no gun"

"I knew it. Knew at the time. Busted musket was in the corner. Oh, hell! Forget it!"

"Can't do that. I'll tell Sarah you're in Yorktown and she'll want you to dinner. You'll come?"

"I'd be obliged."

They were shaking hands when shabby Terry Shea strolled through the batwings. The Irishman's watery eyes were half shut and underscored with smudge-dark circles. He puddled dark streaks of water across the sawdust-strewn floor.

"Shea!"

The man staggered against the bar. "M-Mr. Blake, sir?"

"Damn it, where you been? There's all the goddamn cleanin'—"

But Terry Shea's face had turned sickly green.

"Christ, Mr. Blake, I got to—" the small, wiry fellow shoved off from the bar, stumbling for the back door with hands clamped over his mouth.

Blake shook his head. "Dumb bastard will claim he ate bad food. As if he ever eats. Hell, a bottle of Forty-Rod'll be his supper most nights."

"Heard you dealing with him yesterday," the big man said. "You always ride Shea that rough?"

"Terry's a drunk. You got to ride drunks rough, else they'll—"

"Do me a favor, Blake? Shea, after he upchucks and feels better some, can be a big help to me today. Consider giving him the afternoon off?"

"Huh? Well, sure Lieutenant, whatever you say. Hell, I owe you. Think nothin' of it. Any time."

"This'll likely be the one and only time, but thanks." He lifted his gaze to peer outside over the tops of the batwing doors. "Appears the rain is breaking up. Reckon I'll mosey out back, catch Terry quick as I can now. Be seeing you, Blake." But the big barkeep was watching a bunch of customers troop in and was immediately occupied laying down glasses of strong drink.

"Terry, you in there?" Ryder could see movement through the moon-shaped crescent in the shithouse door. "Terry?"

"Aaargh! Just a minute!" More than a minute elapsed before there at last came a weak: "Ryder? What the hell you want?"

"I'm registered at the Sunflower," the big man called through the cracks. "Want to have a meeting today. Can you round up for me those ranchers who've sold out to Robeson?"

69

"My boss, Blake—"

"You got the day off."

"Hell, Ryder, whyn't you say so?" The door flew open, emitting stink, flies and Terry Shea grinning from ear-to-ear. "What a time!" The wiry Irishman laughed, wiping his red, wet puss with an almost-as-red faded bandana. "Afternoon of no work!" The grin magnified, and gained in brightness. "Plus, by God, a chance to help screw that old son of a bitch enemy of mine, Dick Robeson!"

CHAPTER 7

The clock on the hotel room bureau read five minutes to seven, and Ryder uncrossed his legs, sat up straight, and surveyed the place yet another time. It was a trifle crowded in here, he had to admit. Not knowing how many folks Terry Shea would bring, he'd arranged for three additional chairs from Elmer. That made five in all, plus a bed took up a lot of room besides. Peering across at where Liz sat, he was satisfied. The woman had spent over a half-hour after supper in combing and primping, looked so good as a result that a man wanted to toss her onto the bed and have at her. The flaming hair shone and reflected lamp glow fetchingly. The tanned face and hands radiated health, and all was set off by the modest but modish silk dress.

Well, *maybe* the neckline didn't need to be quite that high. But he'd asked her back at the ranch to trick herself out to put menfolk on her side, and she'd done so. She was pretty as a June bug. Still, when she smiled, the smile seemed nervous. Ryder got to his feet, crossed to her. "No cause to worry, Liz," he told her. "It's going to go all right."

"You think so?"

"Sure as shooting. These old boys Shea promised to bring are the ones most likely in the whole country to side with you. And not just on account of your looks, neither. Knowing Robeson's way of buying up property, there'd have been pressure aplenty put on these men to make them sell to him."

She smoothed her bodice, seeming not to notice the fuller outlining of her breasts. "So, our game tonight is to stoke whatever fires Robeson lit under these men. You figure that even years-old wrongs can stay alive, and hurtful."

"Gal, that's usually the way." There were footfalls in the hall outside. "Hold on. Looks like our company's arriving."

He was ready beside the door when the knocks came, three grouped and a fourth a second later, as had been agreed on with Shea. Ryder swung the panel open and was greeted by three strangers' faces in addition to the Irishman's. "Gents, I'm glad you could make it," he said. "Step right on in."

First over the threshold was a vigorous man of middle age, suited like an Easterner even to a tilted-over-an eye derby. The face under the hat was sunburned brown, and the hands were the gnarled hands of a lifelong ranchman. Following was an old-timer, bearded in gray, gray-haired and of a sickly, gray complexion. Keeping pace with Shea and entering with him last was a man whose most startling feature was absolute hairlessness. No chin whiskers. Not even eyebrows. "Fellers, meet Ryder," Shea said. "And that's Mrs. Kennesaw over by the chair, ain't that c'rect, Ryder?"

Ryder nodded.

"This here's Sander Billings." Shea indicated the man in the derby. "The graybeard over there is Horace Poole, and that's Tom McCracken, bald fella." After the introductions, Shea backed off into a corner by the window, thrust both hands in his pockets, and was quiet.

"Chairs, gents? Make yourselves comfortable." While Liz smiled broadly from her seat, Ryder moved across the room to the bureau where two bottles and a tray of glasses had been set by Elmer when the clerk had made his last trip to the room a half hour before. "We got Cyrus Noble and—let's see, rye whisky here waiting. Anybody got a preference?" Ryder knew that Terry Shea did, but he didn't let himself look in his direction.

"Noble," declared Billings, and McCracken echoed him. Horace Poole wagged his scraggly beard in the direction of the squat bottle containing supposedly genuine Maryland rye. Ryder poured and distributed, making his own choice the Noble. He drank whisky on occasion and remained clear-headed with it. Cold beer was his saloon preference.

"There. To good times." All the men but Shea took long, slow sips. "And now, for what I invited you all for," Ryder continued. "I reckon Terry Shea didn't leave you men exactly in the dark."

Sander Billings leaned forward in his chair,

rested elbows on his brown-gaberdine knees, and pursed his lips. "Well, I don't know, Mr. Ryder, I truly don't. What Shea told me when he came to my house this afternoon was that a man unhappy doing business with Richard Robeson was in town, and that man wanted to make contact with others who'd dealt with Robeson in the past. Now everybody in these parts is aware that two years ago I sold my ranch and moved to town to live off the proceeds. I don't feel Robeson cheated me in any way. I guess that's why I'm a bit confused, coming here."

"What I want to learn about," Ryder said, "is the dirty tactics Robeson tried to pull. In his campaign to buy out the Kennesaw's Rocking K, for instance, I've seen a puncher killed, a raid on the ranchstead, and a slew of cattle slaughtered at pasture. And I've only been at the spread two days. Before my time, of course, Liz, Jess and Cathy Kennesaw's husbands were shot down, and there seems to be a tie-in with their turning down Robeson's purchase offer."

"Do tell? I'd heard about Joe and his brothers' unfortunate end, but didn't make the connection with Richard."

"Richard Robeson." Sander Billings' rock-hard jaw thrust forward. "Mr. Ryder, as far as I'm concerned, Richard Robeson is a sterling gentleman. I'm his friend, you may say, and therefore prejudiced, but I assure you, I wasn't even so much as acquainted with the man at the time he made his offer for my Flying B. As for pressure tricks, he used none whatsoever. His cash bid was generous, but I didn't accept at first—not used to the idea of retiring. *And yet* Richard Robeson was patient. When the following year he renewed the offer, I accepted. I did so well on the deal, I confess, that I can afford to live idle, and can continue so all my days."

"No threats, no gunplay?" Ryder fished in his vest pocket.

"Nothing like that."

Ryder idly fingered a lucifer match. "Well-ll—" The slender stick went between his teeth swiftly. "What do you know?" Liz's gaze was on him, but he ignored it. "Mr. Poole?" He swung to the bearded old-timer.

He was combing blunt fingers through his gray locks, and the flinty eyes were bright. "Horace Poole, yeah, that's me. Well, mister, can't honestly say my doings was different than Billings'. fuss I ain't no *amigo* of Robeson, never was, never will be. He's kinda stuck-up; I drink snakehead whisky for the taste. He wears clothes tailor-made in San Antone, buckskins suit me. But the feller's done me no harm, I'd be a liar to say he did. Was right generous buyin' up m' land, too."

"No fuss?" Ryder wanted to know.

The old-timer sipped his rye. "No fuss."

"Look here," Tom McCracken said. His round bald head caught the lamplight, reflecting dully. "Seems your little party is goin' for naught, Ryder. Ha!" He hoisted his glass at the big man, turned and showed it to Liz Kennesaw as well. "I listen to the gossip. Hang around Josh Pinkerton's barbershop just to soak up the talk. God knows I don't

75

need the shop's trade! But, what I want to say, by God, is that I heerd o' the Kennesaw's troubles, but couldn't rightly figure 'em. Old Dick Robeson done right by me! Waited *three* years for me to make up m' mind, raised the ante, finally, took m'herd off m'hands at a right handsome figure!"

Liz said nothing, Ryder said nothing. In the corner, little Terry Shea simply belched. The three invited visitors studied each other, and alternately the bottoms of three empty glasses.

At last Ryder broke the silence. "Something occurs to me. Each of you men owned a ranch in these parts, then sold out to Richard Robeson. None of you admit to any force on Robeson's part."

"Hell, why *should* we admit any," old Mc-Cracken cackled. It just plain didn't happen that-away, Ryder!"

"Y'old coot, let the feller ask his question!"

"Shit."

"What I think Ryder wants to know," said Liz rising from her seat and gliding between the men to pour herself a shot of Noble, "is, what happened to the other ranchers besides yourselves who sold out to Robeson? I can think of Orville Childress, for one, and I know there were more. Mr. Billings?"

"Far as I've heard, nobody, even them as took their money and bought spreads someplace else, had any hard feelings about Robeson's treatment. Only Joe, Jack and Jamie Kennesaw. Come to think on it, that may say some things about the Kennesaw boys and their women! How—?"

"Meeting over," interrupted Ryder. "Sure was

nice of you gents to stop on by. Don't forget your hats, now. Have a good stroll home."

"Huh?"

"Well, damn if it don't—"

"Goodnight," Liz said. "And again, thanks."

"There," Ryder breathed, shutting the door after the fat backside of Tom McCracken. Then to Terry Shea, "I thought there'd been hard feelings between Robeson and those he bought out."

"'Parently not." The little Irishman shrugged. "Damn it, how should I know, Ryder? I done what you asked, at least, got all them old boys together."

"Yeah. And I thank you for it. But . . . " The big man's words trailed off as he ran something through his mind. "Say, Shea! *You've* got it in for Robeson, from the way you've talked! What's your gripe about the bastard?"

"Me?" Shea reached forth, snagged the rye bottle from the bureau and downed rapidly a series of deep gulps. "What have I got against Mr. Robeson? One thing. This!"

Ryder looked at Liz, she returned his gaze and shrugged. "Damn it, Terry."

"Don't get your ass outa joint, Ryder. Beggin' your pardon, ma'am." Shea finished with a quick burp, paused and grind. "I got the best reason in the world for hatin' Robeson!" The Irishman slammed his hat on and made for the door. "I used to work at the Slash-Diamond-Slash! He went and fired me, the bastard—for drinking!"

Ryder turned from the door and faced Liz Kennesaw's hot gaze. She was refilling her whisky glass from the bottle on the cheap hotel bureau, splashing amber liquid over the rim and sides. He'd never seen the redhead so visibly upset, not even in the heat of yesterday's gunfight at the Rocking K. She tossed the drink back, peeled red lips back from straight white teeth and released a sigh. "Well! I should've known this trip to town and the whole idea of a meeting would turn out a waste!"

Ryder studied her. "Why's that, Liz?"

"Get a bunch of Robeson's lying friends together and what can you expect? Song and dance time at the circus!" She set the glass down and turned, disgust hardening the smooth features which, up until this minute, Ryder had so admired. "*Sure*, Billings, McCracken and Poole have nothing bad to say—" She broke off, snorting.

"A funny thing, Liz. Those men looked like they were telling the truth. I can't explain it, exactly, but I'm inclined to believe that Robeson gave none of them the kind of trouble the Kennesaws have been having. Now, the question is, why?"

"Why you're inclined to believe them?"

"Why their size-up of Richard Robeson don't agree with ours. Hell, everything I've heard from you and Cathy and Jessica makes this one rancher into all devils rolled together. All right, to back that notion we got the dead hand, Lemuel, plus them slaughtered steers. But does it prove Robeson's behind any of it?"

Liz's eyes turned icy. "What are you driving at, Ryder? That all us Kennesaw women are really the liars?" She was pacing back and forth now, wherever the chairs crowding the room admitted passage for her free-swinging skirts. "Well, consider this!" She stopped short directly in front of the big man, stood with hands balled in tiny fists. "Consider Terry Shea! Those *were* Slash-Diamond-Slash punchers in the Elephant yesterday! Now were they or weren't they fixing to trap you like Shea said?"

Ryder shook his head. "Hard to say. Shea is a drunk. Listen, Liz, there's plenty that's funny about your little range war. I got dropped smack in the middle, figured I could help three outnumbered women." The words were harsh, but he had to say them. "Gal, have you told me the whole story?"

"Huh?"

"I asked. Tell me."

The flame-haired woman suddenly slumped, dropped her gaze, let her fists uncoil. "Yes," she said, eyes fixed on the floor. "I have told you everything. Now can I go to my room? I'm tired."

She looked more than tired: exhausted. Ryder himself was restless, his mind racing, but there seemed no more to be got from the woman, not tonight. "Yeah, go ahead. Only remember I want to head back to the Rocking K early."

She slipped through the door and was gone. A minute later he heard sounds through the thin wall, water splashing in a basin, the klunk of kicked-off shoes. When the bed in the next-door room creaked and he knew she'd climbed in, he sat in a chair, chewed a match stick and pictured the woman lying alone in the warm dark.

A half-hour later he was still listening to klunks and squeaks, and decided Liz was more wakeful than she'd reckoned when she'd turned in. He got up silently, took two clean glasses and the Noble bottle from the bureau and eased the door open and himself out into the dimly lit hall. He tried Liz's knob, and when it turned out locked he rapped gently. "Say, I got a little nightcap here."

"Go away."

"What I mean—"

"Go away!"

Ryder shrugged, retraced his steps, replaced the liquor. Then the vague need to think returning, he snatched his wadded-up slicker from the bed and exited.

The night was humid, but most of the clouds had blown away to reveal bright stars. Action continued across the street at the Elephant and Palace, and would till daybreak, but Ryder had had his fill of people for one day. He moved along the boardwalk easily, the unneeded slicker tucked up under his left arm, heading for the livery. Sure, why not check the horses and stow the slicker under the buckboard seat at the same time? Maybe the exercise would get his thoughts going.

Christ, what he'd learned from the trio Shea'd brought turned this whole Rocking K business into a first-class puzzle. Had Richard Robeson a grudge against the Kennesaws? Or were the Rocking K killings and mean tricks not the work of the rancher at all?

If Liz had information, she hadn't passed it

along. Well, he'd be talking to her again in the morning.

The stable's big main door was shut. Ryder made his way along the side down the alley. A lamp burned inside, visible through a single, high window. He was about to pound on the rear door to attract the livery man, but a voice, gruff and low, came from the shadows. "Hold it, Ryder."

Called by name? What the hell—

"Here's a ten-gauge Greener. Make a play and you're a dead man."

"No play." Ryder saw light glint faintly on twin barrels.

"Good. Now walk there! Straight ahead!"

They were at the edge of town. Some tumbledown shanties stood about, forlorn, deserted.

"Inside that 'un! Move!" Ryder watched for a break, but detected none. The man behind the voice looked tall and slim, takable with fists, but the scattergun wouldn't allow that. Shit! Hands half raised, Ryder could only do as told. Maybe once inside he'd be able to spin, turn the tables, get the sword-Bowie out and working.

"Wait! Nigh forgot. Drop your gunbelt and the goddamn short sword. Easy, feller! Move slow!" The words were sinister, but an even more dangerous sound now grabbed attention: a low growl. The hairs on Ryder's neck stiffened. Goosebumps pricked his skin.

"Over by the shack door. Thataway. Now, grab that latchstring."

The snappish snarling burst out again. Inside. A big dog, a bad one.

Ryder felt himself shoved, crashed through the shack door into utter blackness. The dog charged. The door banged shut. The savage growls hurtled toward Ryder. Yet, despite all, he heard clearly from outside: "Easy, just like Mr. Robeson said!"

The dog slammed Ryder, ninety pounds of fur and slashing teeth.

CHAPTER 8

Two things Ryder had learned: the trap was for him, and it was being sprung at Richard Robeson's express, vicious bidding. But the big man had no more time to consider, with the dog hard at him in the dark, abandoned shed. The force of the beast as it crashed into him threw Ryder against the wall, but, thank God, teeth found only air before a sharp kick connected with canine ribs and turned growls to a breathless gasp. Somewhere on the floor, ninety pounds of fury struggled to gather itself, but already Ryder was on the move, groping for the door, finding it wedged tightly from the outside. No use. Out there were his six-gun and sword; in here he had only a pair of hands. He whirled—not a second to lose—and came up wrapping his left forearm with his bundled slicker.

When the dog leaped again, it fastened teeth into the tough rubbered cloth, but failed to find flesh. Relief flooded Ryder. But only for a split second. Lightning-like, the dog released its jaws, fell back, and then dove for the big man's legs. Hearing scuffling, he lashed out with a boot, felt the sharp impact. The dog's head snapped around and a rash of snarls erupted.

"There, you son of a bitch!" Ryder's mind raced. If the dog's razor-sharp teeth found his throat, he was a goner. He had to keep the beast away, somehow, anyhow. Hit it. Hit it hard as hell. Ryder's hands cast about, came up with a plank that, though splintered and rough, was at least a solid weapon. Another leap. Ryder's club powered into the dog's forelegs, upsetting it, and from the sound of things, inflicting pain. But, judging from the sound, another mad scramble was occurring, to be followed by another leap. The jaws clamped on his booted lower leg. Ryder hammered down with his plank powerfully, inflicting more damage, but the dog was already up on hind legs and went for Ryder's throat.

The wrapped left arm rammed the dog's blunt snout. Hanging on to a mouthful of slicker, the animal clawed with hind legs at Ryder's unprotected midsection. The big dog's bite lanced through the cloth of the slicker and Ryder felt blood trickling from the painful wound. It was Ryder's turn. In a surge of superhuman effort, he somehow managed to shake the gigantic dog loose.

It snapped again at the man's leg, drawing more blood. Hurt raged through Ryder—searing, brutal hurt. And then dog and man were down on the dirt floor, rolling. One minute the snarling, slicker-chewing dog superior, the next minute positions reversed with the struggling, swearing man on top. Ryder scissored the brute with his legs, the dog

84

squirmed free. Ryder staggered to his feet realizing angrily only too late that he'd lost the club. The growling grew louder in the blackness. His strength was failing, ringing ears seriously hampering his action.

While the dog only seemed to grow stronger—or more blood-mad— with each attack.

Ryder lashed out a booted foot but only kicked air. The beast had dodged. The shadowy hunk seemed to fill the shanty.

The dog leaped.

With the quickness of desperation, Ryder thrust his padded arm up to protect his upper body. He felt the impact of the airborne animal. Its rancid hot breath stung his nostrils. The chomping teeth shredded the slicker, bits of fabric flew like windblown thistledown. Ryder's strength was ebbing; shards of pain split his bursting lungs. The big man's hand combed the huge dog's underbelly. The beast still hung high against him, snapping and growling. Ryder's hand moved downward. Suddenly he knew what to do to save himself. His fingers found the naked testicles. With the last of his strength he clutched, twisted, yanked.

The dog's anguish gave vent in a mighty howl. When its teeth parted from his wrapped left wrist Ryder exulted. He yanked again. The dog was harmless now, but for how long? It tried to break free. But, encountering more pain, flopped helplessly on its side.

With a last mighty heave Ryder gripped and ripped. With a great tear of skin, the bloody testicles came away in his clenched fingers.

He dropped the trophy on the gore-muddied floor. Suddenly the dog was just a ceaselessly writhing, howling, agony-racked ball of fur, bleeding freely from between hind legs. Ryder didn't bother to kick the animal and groped for the door instead. He beat at the door with all his strength.

The door gave with a splintering crash. The big man stepped through and outside into a fresh, silvered land. Moonlight flooded a deserted road. The man who'd jumped him was long gone, doubtless back to town. But Ryder's weapons lay on the ground. He bent to scoop up the well-worn gun belt, holstered Smith & Wesson, and the lopped-off sabre.

Stumping on legs still a might shaky, Ryder made for the hotel, the howls of the injured dog turning to wimpers as its strength ebbed away.

At his rap, Liz jerked her door open. Daybreak's gray light shone behind her, highlighting the flaming hair and yellow silk dress. "Ready?" Ryder queried.

"Yes, I—My God, what happened to you?"

Ryder looked down at himself. The shirt had been ripped by the dog's teeth and claws; the vest and pants were covered with bloody dirt. The cuts on his hands were gruesome, although he'd cleaned up as much as possible at the washstand in his room. The mirror there had told him his face was scratched and bruised, also. A mess. A real mess. But at least he knew who'd done it.

"Got me a present from a dog lover. Richard

Robeson."

"What?" Concern was written in her eyes. She reached out and touched his bruised cheek.

He grinned. "And you're off the hook, gal. I know now for sure Robeson's out to get you. And me, too, because I'm backing your plays."

"Will you—"

"Will I go on working for you? Hell, yes. But we got to go now. I got the buckboard waiting." He clamped his teeth on the stub of a chewed lucifer. "Was up early, talked with Terry Shea. Got me an idea, and a damn good one, where we ought to go next."

Ryder lay stretched behind a mesquite bush, telescope to his eye, concentrating. It was hot in the sun, damned hot. But there was no shade, not on this range, not within shouting distance of the Slash-Diamond-Slash. Men came and went about the yard of Robeson's ranchstead, filing between the painted, well-kept buildings. Occasionally, one or more rode out on horses. But not *the* man, Robeson himself. Well, he couldn't stay indoors forever, could he?

Ryder wondered. He'd wormed into position hours ago, and was by now getting cramps in his cramps.

Shit! The bastard had to show or he'd wasted the day. He'd have done better helping the Kennesaw women rope and drag dead steers into a pile and burn the carcasses before the rot set in. Of course, they were good horsewomen, and could make out themselves. Had before he'd dropped along, would still be doing so after he'd pulled stakes and gone.

But he didn't aim to go, not yet. He had to stop Robeson, and to stop him, he had to talk with the man. At least, that's what his plan called for.

Ryder was sun-baked, insect-chewed, and badly needed to pee. The sun's position told the time: mid-afternoon. Riding up to Robeson's doorstep made no sense, not after last night. Any bastard who'd throw a man to a vicious dog wouldn't hesitate to shoot and ask questions later. There were too many gunmen on the place, as Terry Shea had warned. But more important was the disclosure by the former Slash-Diamond-Slash man of his old employer's habit.

Then, appearing big as you please through the leveled 'scope, the gray-haired man Ryder had seen at the hotel appeared now on his own porch, booted and spurred for going horseback. The swarthy face was as unreadable as two nights ago. Robeson paused and adjusted his buttermilk-white, Dakota-creased Stetson. And sure enough, in the next minute a small figure bounded out of the house and down the steps. Hatted, too, and wearing miniature versions of the rancher's boots, the boy fidgeted eagerly.

Terry Shea's description was unbelievably accurate.

The son looked nothing like the father, being sandy-haired and frail. Toothpick limbs failed to fill out his clothes, and the kid was pale, mighty pale. And according to Shea, he was outdoors a lot, too, usually in company of the small man, Shorty, who acted as a bodyguard. Except on these rides with the father.

Once daily when he was home, Robeson would take his nine-year-old son out riding. As a result the kid rode well enough, but never got to leave the Slash-Diamond-Slash spread. Not on these excursions. Not ever.

It was as if the kid's existence were being kept secret, although plenty of folks around Yorktown knew about him. Another peculiarity of the mysterious, wifeless Robeson. One that Ryder meant to exploit.

The big man was already worming backward through the dry grass, telescope pocketed for the time being, shirt and vest getting dirtied. He'd picketed his horse just back of a rise, and when the Robesons mounted, he needed to be ready as well. Shea claimed the rancher wasn't locked into any particular route; man and boy might trot off in any direction. As Ryder watched, a wrangler led a big dun and a slighter brown-and-white pinto from the stable. Saddled, restless, and eager to move. Words were exchanged as the rancher was mounting. Quick as a cat the kid vaulted into the saddle, too, and reined the pinto around with a practiced hand.

Here they came. There was a brush-choked gully between Ryder and the mounted pair, and they turned to skirt it, bearing south now, into the blazing sun. But Ryder had scouted the country and knew they wouldn't go without shade long. A creek cut the land about a mile ahead, a creek with banks grown up full of cottonwoods and willows. That had to be the reason for this route. Ryder slipped over the rise and up to the Rocking K chestnut. The horse stopped cropping grass and looked at him.

"Ho, feller. Ready to move?" He placed his boot in the stirrup, lifted. Adjusted the Winchester boot to ride comfortably under his leg, the sabre sheath at his belt. "Let's go!" And with a touch of the big man's heels the chestnut moved out, loping parallel to the gully, but out of view. Robeson would spot him soon enough, Ryder figured. But only after he was all set up and ready.

Ryder sat the chestnut behind a big sycamore, screened from the trail by serviceberry and clumped sage. The creek burbled behind him and from up the trail came the patient clop-clop of approaching hoofs. It had to be the Robesons, father and son.

He slid the Smith & Wesson from its holster, broke the weapon, checked the five loaded .44 chambers. Snapped it closed, eared the hammer back.

Robeson's dun trotted into view, the boy on the pinto nearly on its heels. The rancher appeared stern, wrapped in his thoughts, certainly not enjoying himself in the kid's company. From the wide, thin lips a black cheroot dangled, and once a minute a round cloud of smoke escaped to spiral upward in the breezeless air. The pair were nearly opposite Ryder's position. The big man rose in his stirrups, opened his mouth.

"Hold it right there!" Ryder's voice rang clearly, crisp rather than loud so as to be understood the first time across the distance. Richard Robeson reined in sharply and the kid followed suit. "That's good." At Ryder's urging the chestnut danced forward, bringing him out of the brush and directly into Robeson's path.

"You!"

"You know me, then," the big man snapped.

"The boys said I'd recognize Ryder by the mustache, the short sword slung at the belt." The rancher seemed grim but unafraid, at least for himself. Ryder had noted, though, that he'd managed to position the dun he straddled in front of the kid.

"You don't want trouble that could hurt the younker."

Robeson barked, "I don't."

"We got to parley, is all. Here." Ryder lowered the barrel of the six-gun, light glinting on the plated steel. Then with a flourish he holstered the weapon. "Showing my good faith."

The rancher nodded, folded his own hands over his saddle horn.

"We'll talk this way, no need to dismount."

Robeson nodded again. His brow curled into a frown, and the thin lips tightened. He didn't like his fix one bit. "I don't know what you want to discuss, Ryder. We're on opposite sides in a war."

"Is that so? War, you say? Just because you want the Kennesaw women's spread?"

"It's the way I see it."

"That's why you hired away or drove off or killed all the Rocking K hands? And what about Joe, Jack and Jamie Kennesaw? Weren't they gunned down at your orders?"

He glanced at the boy. "I admit nothing."

Ryder leaned forward in the saddle. "Then, there's the cattle. A couple dozen head, night before last, their throats cut and left to rot on Rocking K range. *No* kinds of lives matter to you, do they Robeson? Not your own men's, I saw that in their last raid."

Robeson's black eyes glittered like tiny chips of coal. "In war there are always casualties."

"I could've got killed in that raid. I could've got bushwhacked the day I saw you in town. I could've died easy, chomped to bits last night by a god-damned trained dog! You don't look surprised, Mr. Robeson, that those things happened."

The cheroot in Robeson's teeth burned short. His eyes shone like the glowing ash. He raised a hand slowly, rolled the butt between his fingers, dropped it.

A spat grain of tobacco followed the flung cheroot to the ground. "You want to know something, Ryder? You live risky. You work for the Kennesaw widows. You thought of quitting?"

"I ain't a quitter. But here's one more question. Why the rough stuff with the Rocking K? Other ranches you bought on the square, for fair prices, keeping good feelings with the folks."

Richard Robeson sneered, his hard eyes fixed Ryder like a snake's. Hatred boiled in the man. Hatred of Ryder, just a feller passing through, stopped to lend a hand to some hard-pressed widows. But it wasn't crazy hate, not altogether. Robeson wanted the big man eliminated, out of the way.

Ryder tilted the black hat back on his head, gave a grim smile. "Well, nice palavering with you, Mr. Robeson. Since I ain't hightailing, we might be seeing each other." He kneed the chestnut into motion, rode around the rancher and up the trail. Cocked a finger at the kid on the pinto. "So long, sonny."

And when screened by the trees and out of view, he spurred for the Rocking K.

Ryder ate supper in the Kennesaw kitchen, listening to the women talk. Not much learned in the conversation with Robeson, he had little to say. Liz had told the others about the dog, Ryder's scrapes and scratches, the uneventful buggy ride home from town.

After the meal, they all sat around the fire, with clothes-mending. Christ! Butter wouldn't melt in these three's mouths, and coolest of all was Jessica. He'd attempted to signal the black-haired beauty, but there was this very interesting torn and out-at-the-toe knit sock.

"Well, good evening, ladies." The ancient clock on the mantel was chiming eight. Ryder wasn't as much tired, as bored.

The outhouse and then the bunkhouse. He didn't bother with a lantern, simply stripped to balbriggans in the hot, moist dark. The tick on the bunk was soft.

Not long after he dozed off, he was awakened by the door creaking open. The quick hand darted, brought the six-gun from the bedpost-slung holster.

A shadowed form half-filled the doorway.

"Oh, don't shoot, Ryder, please," the soft, sweet voice cooed. "I-It's only me. Cathy."

CHAPTER 9

"Cathy?"

Ryder could see her walking slowly toward him. The window admitted just enough light to make out her white nightshift, pale face, softly shimmering blond hair. God! The likeness to Holly! Holly's locks, too, had formed a pale-gold halo, hung long in back, and swept seductively forward over cream-smooth shoulders when she'd bend low over him. Like now.

But, this wasn't Holly. Holly was dead. Here in the darkened Rocking K bunkhouse a different woman held finger to fully, beestung lips, cautioned him to stay calm and quiet.

"Yes, it's me," she whispered urgently. "I came to visit. Don't care that it's late, and Jess and Liz are long abed. I got a yearnin'."

She bent still lower over Ryder and chucked him playfully under the chin. "Mister, you know what I'm sayin'. And I just know you got to be a real man. I been watchin' Jessica since that first day. There's roses in her cheeks again, and she walks more, well, swayin', don't you see? Like when she still had Jamie to pleasure her." Ryder thought he detected a sniffle. "Poor Jamie. Poor Jack." In filtered moonglow, tears glistened on the woman's cheeks. "But when gals' menfolk die, life does have to go on, don't you reckon?"

"I—"

"All I'm askin' for is what you already gave Jess. And Liz. I know Liz spent the night with you in town."

"But we never—"

Sobs were shaking Cathy, the straw tick, the entire bunk. "Oh, what the hell—" When she kissed him he kissed back, hard. He found her tongue thrusting into his mouth. And meanwhile fingers, smooth, cool fingers were at his undershirt buttons.

The cloth fell away. She shucked him like a cob of corn. "It's been so long, so long . . . " She drew her hands from him, stood to pull her flimsy shift up and over her head. It whispered to the floor.

It was her only garment. Naked, her silhouette in the gloom gleamed faintly. Large, deep breasts the shape of melons, ripe hips, slim-flowing thighs quivered, undulated.

She dropped on him.

"My, you got you a nice thing. Bet it tastes just fine."

Before Ryder could say a word she'd wrapped her lips around his member. And damned if the tonguing wasn't just as nice as when she'd been doing it in his mouth a minute ago. Nicer! He could feel the pulsing in his stalk, and the blood

96

hammering in his brain as well—tiny triphammers of delight.

She took time out to speak. "I got me a better idea. Look, you're all up and ready! Try this!" And his railspike organ was cased in hands deft from kneading bread dough. Teasing, tempting him to come right then and there over her fist and fingers, Cathy Kennesaw pumped and mangled. As she labored, she bent low, and the full, deep breasts brushed his chest like feather pillows. He twisted, made the effort, and his lips captured a nipple. He lapped eagerly. Her breath gusted, and he raised the tempo. "Good," she cried, "it feels so good!"

Ryder put an arm up to trap her head and pull her face close for a kiss that galvanized. She shivered and gasped. The woman hung on with arms and legs both, and a silky thigh pressed to his groin, grinding.

"Mustn't hurt," she mumbled, tearing her mouth away.

He cut her off again, gluing his lips once more to hers. Below, her hands continued their magic, fingers spidering maddeningly over his crotch, thighs, belly. His mushroom tip throbbed at a caress to its underside, and his response was immediate. He snaked his own hand to her private place, felt the moistness, rubbed a finger in it. Probing, he parted her, brought his manhood within range, let her aim it. At the touch, a wild grinding seized her, and she moaned aloud on penetration.

"Yes!" she panted. "Yes!"

COLE WESTON

On top now and in control, Ryder plunged and bottomed, felt her clasp loosen and his ramrod tingle. "Screw me, Ryder, screw me!" He did so, powerfully. "Harder! Harder!" she wailed. He bottomed another time, drew back, repeated.

The woman twitched frantically and squealed. Her orgasm was on her and she rocked in rhythm. Ryder nearly lost contact as her pelvis gyrated, but he forced her against him and threw weight on her, pinned her, continuing to grind all the while. Relentless now, he managed to raise at each stroke, heightening sensation by increasing friction. Catching on, the woman rolled with him, bucking, twisting.

"Fuck me, Ryder, fuck me! Oh, fuck me some more!"

The big man did so.

Pounding with a fury born of too-long delay, the big man's gristle stroked, probed, drove. Cathy, crushed to the thin straw tick, lifted the best she could to the onslaught, grinding her entire lower body. Her fingernails dug Ryder's nipples, bringing him to peak. And herself as well, a second shattering orgasm tore a cry from her throat and she thrashed the harder.

The last moment was approaching. Ryder slacked his speed, then plunged with new energy, wringing every drop of her juice to oil his passage. Then his own fluid sprang boiling, waves of sensation lifting, hurling him from side to side in a rush of fulfillment. He went limp, fell across the woman, groaning. The groan was muffled between pillowing breasts.

Before he could roll free, he felt the woman's grip at his scrotum. "Wait! Don't pull out! Just a little. . ."

He let her do it. Using what rigidity he retained by grasping his root, she worked speedily to give herself more pleasure. It didn't take long. Lifting gently to make room, he could see the length of his body to the small, pale hand a-flutter.

"All right?"

"Y-yes, all—Oh! Oh! *Oh* !"

Cathy Kennesaw twitched, then twitched again. Then an all-consuming spasm took her, carried her along to the highest peak yet, held her there while sobs husked from her and she loosed him at last, hands and love nest, too.

He lay still, venting a sigh.

"You're so good," she breathed. Motionless now, she was wedged next to him in the narrow bunk. Damned if the touch of her warm skin wasn't having its effect, causing him to grow again!

"No slouch, yourself." His cupped palm crept to a puckered areole, the bud at its center, soft in the woman's afterglow. It didn't stay that way. Shifting to give better access to her breasts, Cathy let both globes hang forward, fill his hands. Swelling rapidly, the nipples he massaged now turned bullet-hard. Simultaneously, to his delight, the thigh he'd pressed between hers received a warm flood of drool from her pulsing cave.

"Ready again? My goodness!" She wriggled as she giggled.

"Here!"

Heaving onto her, Ryder drew the woman and

impaled her. Sinking blossom and shaft till he bottomed, the big man also bore up, sending that iron-bar rigidity into exquisite sliding contact with her tab. "Aah! Aah! Aa-aah!" She tightened, clasped internally, then released. Her buttocks pounded. He was building as well as she, and the urgency pulsing in his groin told him to hurry.

The two exploded together, both gushing feeling as well as fluid. Both bodies bucked, shuddered, then all movement ceased.

They rested, legs entwined, sighing as their racing hearts slowed. They fell asleep.

Later awakening, hearing her murmur, "Good, Ryder, good. God, oh, so good!"

He dreamed of Holly. Holly of the golden hair. Cathy of the golden hair. Himself.

Frowning, Ryder stepped from the dim barn into morning sunlight. It would be taking a few more days for his lame bay's leg to mend. Shit! Best piece of horseflesh on the place, and still unfit to ride.

Poor animal.

For that matter, poor Rocking K.

Poised in the building's narrow ribbon of shade, the big man squinted eastward. Smoke still rose from yesterday's bonfire of dead cattle, and a disgusting stench drifted across the range. Worse, the carcasses weren't destroyed entirely. He'd need to be riding out with the women in the buckboard, cans of kerosene loading the back end.

A hell of a thing. But at least, according to Liz at breakfast, there'd been no sign of further stock-killing. Maybe Robeson was planning different mischief. From their creekside meeting on the Slash-Diamond-Slash, Ryder hadn't learned much about the rancher. But he *had* seen Richard Robeson wasn't one to give up.

Ryder glanced over at the house. No sign of the women yet. A few minutes more to ponder their mysterious enemy.

Robeson had a deep grudge against the Kennesaws. No telling why, but there *was* telling how far he'd likely go. All the way. To force sale of the Rocking K he'd sacrifice effort, money, lives. But for Liz, Cathy and Jessica to cut and run now would leave them broke. They wouldn't let all they'd slaved so hard for be taken.

And Ryder wasn't about to allow it, either. Not after last night. Cathy was more like Holly than he'd imagined, alike in more than looks. She had inner toughness, courage. Jess had it, too, and of course there was Liz. These women didn't deserve to lose. Husbands murdered, they'd walked through hell, but bounced back fighting.

Trouble was, they couldn't do it themselves anymore.

There was battling Robeson and the ranch work besides. Ryder couldn't be everywhere at once. He'd been trying, God knew, but just falling further behind. The house needed fortifying, and that meant carpentry work. The stock on the range needed attention. And more.

The females were coming. As they crossed from the house, he could see that today they'd dressed alike: jeans stuffed into boots, checked shirts,

101

Stetsons. Liz, in the lead, was pulling on tough gloves. She carried a lasso, and apparently aimed to cut out broncs.

He could recognize now what there was about Jess's walk. A languid sureness of self and her worth as a woman. Now Cathy had it, too.

Since last night.

Ryder grinned, shook his head. "Howdy."

"Howdy to you." Liz shook out a loop. Cathy and Jess studied various things, the ground, the buildings, sky. "Sleep well?"

"Fine."

"Good. We got work aplenty. Jess, Cathy, you—

"Let it rest a minute," Ryder said. "I got a piece to speak."

"Oh?"

He fished a matchstick, studied the red sulphur end as he spoke. "We need more help on the place. Liz, you got to think about hiring more hands."

She laughed. "Think about it! That's a good one! Every cowpoke in this country knows what Robeson's putting out in the way of news. That he pays half again our wages. That Rocking K hands seem to follow Kennesaws into the grave. Don't you think we've tried like hell to get and keep good men?"

"You said before you been trying. I can see the problems. But will you give me the go-ahead to try again? Got me an idea."

"Ryder. . .Oh, all right."

Ryder grinned, popped the lucifer between his teeth. "Good, then, I'll start today." He winked at Cathy, thought about it, decided he'd better wink at

Jessica too. "First, though, let's go fire them carcasses. I'll take the rope."

He took it, shook out a big loop as he made for the corral.

"Make this fast, I got to go to town."

CHAPTER 10

Damn, he thought, surveying the falsefront-lined Yorktown street as he rode in. *Every time I come to this place it smells. And today's worse than ever.*

Unless it was the stink of the burning steer carcasses clinging in his nostrils. It had been a rough morning's work.

"Whoa!"

With the Elephant still a block away Ryder reined tight to the boardwalk. A lurching Studebaker wagon rolled past, heavily laden with ranch supplies. For the Slash-Diamond-Slash? Had to be. There were no more large spreads nearby except the Kennesaws'. Could that be the bulk of Robeson's problem, that the Rocking K was the last ranch he didn't own? Ryder didn't believe it. There was something else to the bastard's orneriness, something secret. He'd bet his britches on it.

But what?

"Hey, Ryder! Got a minute?" Terry Shea called.

"Yeah, Shea. Get your ass over!" Ryder sat tall

on the chestnut, grinning, as the drunk dodged some light buggy traffic getting across the street. Just the feller he wanted to see.

"Ryder, I don't feel so good!" And Shea looked as if he didn't. The clothes had been slept in, and were littered with tiny bits of hay and horseshit. He held his slouch hat to his chest with trembling hands. "I got to have a drink."

"And?"

"And I seen you. Ridin' in. Sight for sore eyes."

"I'm supposed to pay for your booze, Shea?"

"You're m'friend, ain't you?"

"Sure."

"Let me tell you what happened. Y'know that tinhorn dandy, hangs out mostly over to the Elephant?"

Ryder frowned. "Young feller? Frock coat, ruffled shirt? Squints a lot?"

"That's the one! Well, he's out to get me. He was playin' cards last night and lost. Lost big. I was there o' course, just hangin' around, not in the game or nothin', just—"

"This feller?"

"Name's Jason. Jason Kyle. A mean son of a bitch if there ever was one. Nigh as bad as Robeson, even has run with Robeson sometimes, been out to the Slash-Diamond-Slash."

"He blamed you because he lost?"

"Claimed I musta been passin' signals to the other players. Shit, I had to light out through the Elephant's damn back door. Ain't been back since."

"What about your job?"

"Screw the job. I got my skin to think of."

Ryder was still grinning. He took a lucifer, popped it between his teeth. "Scared to go back to the Elephant. Out of work on that account. We got things to talk about, Shea. Buy you a drink over at the Palace?"

Terry Shea beamed. "Don't mind if I do."

An hour later Ryder sauntered over to the Elephant. He had Shea where he wanted him: pledged to stay sober, outfitted in brand-spanking-new puncher's togs, on his way by livery plug out to the Rocking K. A valuable new hand? Maybe. In the big man's opinion it was even likely.

The wiry boozer knew Robeson well, had worked quite a while at the Slash-Diamond-Slash. Hell, Ryder had already used Shea's information, locating Robeson out on horseback with his son. Robeson's surliness wasn't Terry's fault. The man was bitter medicine, simply best spat out, not swallowed.

By sending Shea right out to the ranch he could get him started working today. Also get the Irishman away from the bottles, any temptation he might encounter to celebrate his new status.

Ryder pushed through the batwings into the saloon.

"There you are, Blake! How do?"

Blake, beet-red and sweating under the portrait of the naked pink lady, swung to face the newcomer. His face split in a grin. "Ryder! A great day! Lookit!" Patrons crowded the bar three deep. A couple of extra barmen had been brought in, and both were on the run dispensing beer, crackskull, and the "stone fence" house special—a shot of rye in a glass of cider.

A regular party, as Blake soon said. "We're throwin' us a winding, by God, lieutenant! My Jenny's birthday's today! Hell, you remember the date!"

But Ryder didn't, not right away. There'd been a lot on his mind, visiting Robeson, burning steer carcasses, getting the town drunk on the Rocking K payroll. He considered. Let's see, mid-summer . . . Yes, Blake was correct. And, hell, why wouldn't he be? Little Jenny was *his* daughter.

"Six years old, man, six years old today!" Blake was bawling over the din made by the drinkers. "You helped my wife deliver the baby, lieutenant, and now the baby's six! Ever'body drink up!"

Blake had tipped more than a few glasses of his own crackskull. "That's the what-for of this party?" Ryder asked, gesturing.

"Drinks on the house! What'll *you* be having, Lieutenant Ryder? Beer?"

"Tall and cool." A long-necked bottle was un-corked, set in front of the big man, flooding suds. "Cheers," he said, taking a comfortable pull.

"Cheers!" roared Blake. Then: "Hey, boys, listen here!" A few heads turned along the bar. "I want you-all to meet Lieutenant Ryder!" Christ, but the man's voice was loud! "The lieutenant midwifed m' little Jenny, he did, one rainy Vir-ginia day! Six little old years back! Yessir!"

"To old friends." An old codger in ragged chaps lifted his glass. Ryder raised his own, smiled agreeably.

"Hell, yeah! Delivered the kid? I'll drink to that."

"Another round, by God!"

"Make mine Forty-Rod!"

The crowd was getting in the spirit. Ryder didn't mind celebrations, but one reason he was in the Elephant was to scout punchers for the Rocking K. In the free-drink frenzy, it looked like he'd picked a God-awful bad time. The only sober face visible was at the rear table: Jason Kyle sat as usual, shuffling cards. But the lone-wolf tinhorn was worthless as a recruit. Too close to Robeson. The Palace Saloon up the street had to have patrons, maybe some of them on the outs with Robeson. Worth a try, Ryder decided, draining his beer.

"Lieutenant! You headin' off?" The big man found his way blocked by the beefy form of Blake. The saloonman leaned forward, thick arms folded across his apron. "Hey, we was talking this morning, me and my wife, Sarah. She wanted to know why I hadn't fetched you to dinner. I said, you ain't too often to town. But you're to town today! So come on over to our house, Lieutenant! I ain't no mean drunk. I already stopped tipping 'em for today. Time I get home to Sarah and little Jenny, I'll be judge-sober and preacher-pure."

"Well—"

"Make Sarah plumb delighted, seeing you again, Lieutenant. Like me, she's grateful, powerful grateful you stopped that day you heard her screaming in the cabin. And don't you want to see Jenny? You ain't seen her since Virginia."

Suddenly Ryder *did* want to see Jenny. The infant he'd midwifed all those years ago, when things were bad, all right, but before they'd gone utterly to hell for him. Six years back, Holly was still alive. Lovely Holly. His promised bride for when the War got over.

If not for the renegades, he and Holly would have wed, had a kid now, maybe, of their own. Not quite six yet, of course, but . . .

Blake leaned close. "Aw, c'mon, Lieutenant Ryder. My Sarah's a great cook. Killed a goose for the celebrating. There'll be apples, dressing, and all the fixings."

"I'll come."

"The house is at town's edge, down by the creek. Six o'clock?"

"I'll find it. Just got me some business to tend to first." He saluted. Blake did too.

Ryder made for the batwings, turned to view the rowdy crowd a final time.

Jason Kyle wasn't at his favorite table. Ryder shrugged.

Maybe the man had gone for a piss. You got to go, you got to go.

As Ryder passed the hotel, a familiar horse stood at the rail, rein-thrown, head down, motionless. A bit lathered, as if recently ridden hard.

Richard Robeson's dun.

Ryder's thoughts were interrupted when a dandy in a frock coat ran down the hotel steps. Slim and youngish. Kept his face hidden with a low-tipped Stetson. Jason Kyle? Likely, Ryder reckoned.

Probably working for Robeson too.

He crossed the street, ending up in front of the barber shop.

Should he take a shave? Ryder wondered. Put on a good face for Sarah Blake and her child?

He shoved the door open and a bell tinkled. "Yessir?"

"Shave, trim. Hot towel, Bay Rum, the works, barber. I'm going to a party!"

Ryder mounted the chair.

"Kidnapped?"

"Kidnapped!"

"Good God! When?" Ryder, just inside the front door of the tiny house, stood jolted with surprise, muscles in his jaw working under the taut skin.

"About a half-hour ago, Mr. Ryder." Sarah Blake was weeping into a handkerchief, her short pale-brown hair mussed, eyes red, nose running. Blake himself, purple-faced, stood beside her in the cozy parlor, clenching and unclenching ham-like fists.

"I tried to find you, Lieutenant," the miserable father growled. "Even before we sent for the sheriff. Couldn't find you no place."

"Under a hot towel, damn it, dead to the world. No matter. I'll get your little Jenny back. You say Sheriff Claymore was here?"

"He wasn't. Ain't come yet, though it's been—"

Blake tugged a big Ingersol from his pocket, eyes squinting through his own tears. "God, it's been a hell of a while."

Ryder nodded. "We'll work without the lawman. What did exactly happen?"

"A gang of—"

"Only two men, Gus." The woman's control had somewhat returned, and she now spoke with an icy calm.

"Busted in."

"They knocked. Right gentle, too. I answered the door, Gus. That's natural enough, most days I do it dozens of times. Who'd ever suppose that this time—"

Gus Blake glared at his wife and ground his teeth. "Armed to the skin, I reckon, shootin' irons and knives."

Sarah Blake interrupted again. "They wore the usual six-guns, just like everybody. Well, not everybody back in Virginia, but everybody in these parts. And their bandanas were red, although mighty faded from overmuch washing."

"That's it? That's all?" Ryder wanted to know. He turned the big Smith &Wesson over in his hands. It checked out loaded, ready. He tried the sword-Bowie in its sheath. It slid easily.

"Well—"

"Sarah, you were the one home when it happened, did you say? Gus hadn't got here yet?"

"Not from the Elephant, no. I was here alone with Jenny, Mr. Ryder, like I am a lot, Gus's work being what it is. When I opened the door the two men standing there was real polite, said they wanted to find the Blake place. I told them my name, and just then Jenny toddled in from the kitchen. Stood by the wing chair, right over there, the one with the antimacassar."

"Jenny's shy, you see," she continued, sniffling again. " 'Is this your gal, Jenny?' the big stranger asked. When I said 'Yes,' the littlest of the jaspers ran over, and grabbed her up. She started crying. I tried to fight, but got knocked down. The big man pulled his gun. Told me not to follow outside. They went. They had 'em horses waiting, and they jumped on and rode off. With Jenny across the little one's pommel, squealing fit to bust! Oh, God!"

Footsteps rattled on the porch and the door flew open. "What's goin' on?" Sheriff Bat Claymore strode into the room. He paused to cast the pinkish eyes around curiously. When he moved again he waddled, crossing to the weeping woman as if Ryder and Gus Blake weren't even there. "Miz Blake? I hear there's some trouble?"

Gus Blake shoved forward, the bushy brows over his eyes working. "Kidnap, sheriff. My young'un, Jenny. 'Twas two fellers, one big and one small, and—"

"How small?" it suddenly occurred to Ryder to ask. An idea had just started to buzz in his brain. Maybe, just maybe.

Sarah blake pondered a minute, her mouth bracketed with lines of strain. "Why, real small, Mr. Ryder. Almost as small as a midget I seen once in a circus."

"Shorty!"

"Huh?"

Bat Claymore was stuffing his pipe. Tobacco granules spotted his shirt. Several clung to his polished star. "Strangers, were they? On-the-dodge owlhoots, they musta been."

"Shorty!" Ryder repeated. "Little jasper only so high. Rides for the Slash-Diamond-Slash! You've seen him Blake. Hell, the one time I saw him it was in the Elephant."

"Why, yeah, I know who you mean!"

The sheriff muttered, "Be dark in a couple hours. Get a posse together in the morning. Cold trail by then—"

"Blake," Ryder said, "pack a carpetbag, get hold of a buggy. Sarah's going to the Rocking K, where she'll be safe."

"Wait! I just remembered something!" Sarah's voice piped, high, excited. She was wringing her hands.

Bat Claymore wandered through the door and outside. "Clues . . . tracks . . . "

"Remembered what?" Ryder wanted to know.

"Something the big jasper said. He talked mean, real mean. He told me, 'Tell Ryder to clear out. If he does you get the gal back.' What does it mean, Mr. Ryder? My God, what does it mean?"

Gus Blake bunched his fists. "Who in hell wants to get at you, Ryder? Wants it bad enough to do this thing?"

"I'm trailing after them. Get you a bronc, Blake, and you can come. Move!"

"Oh!" Sarah Blake staggered and nearly collapsed. She kept from falling by clutching at the corner bible stand.

"No, wait!" Ryder snapped, seeing it. "Gus, there's a better way. You go with Sarah, take her to the Kennesaws'."

The woman looked grateful through her sheer haggardness. Gus Blake's shaggy brows lifted, and he slammed his fist hard into his palm.

"I'll get Jenny back, Blake. Bet on it."

The chestnut was in the street, rested, and the canteen slung on the saddle was topped off full. Ryder's Winchester waited in its boot, oiled, deadly.

"Good luck, Lieutenant!"

"Mr. Ryder, God bless!"

The big man crossed the yard in long-legged, loping strides. He vaulted to the saddle.

"Ryder."

He raised his hand in a final wave, then wheeled and spurred.

The chestnut made dust.

CHAPTER 11

Open prairie under a high, bright sky, a few mare's-tail clouds making wisps and a buzzard soaring. The road under the horse blurred as Ryder used spurs, whip-swung reins and growled curses to urge the animal on. The horse responded willingly. The road north out of Yorktown ran arrow-straight across the flat, and at the end of the road, Ryder knew, he'd find the Slash-Diamond-Slash.

If he could overtake little Jenny Blake's kidnappers before they reached the ranch he could head them off, maybe. But then what? He'd know for sure where they were headed, that's about all. He wasn't about to risk gunplay when the kid could get hurt. There was no way he would.

The road dipped. The chestnut charged down into the broad natural dish and up the far side, dust flying at its heels. No one could be seen ahead. Only grass, occasional mesquite clumps and the ever-unwinding road. He let the gelding slow down, stop to blow, but soon was moving fast again, trying to make up the time. The pair had a half-hour's start.

Here's where Terry Shea's knowledge would have been of use, but there was no help available. Terry would be at the Rocking K by now, likely put to work shoveling horse shit.

"Hi, horse, hi! Go boy!" Ryder urged. The chestnut just ran.

As the horse raced, so did Ryder's mind. To think that he was to blame for the little kid's danger! Sure, Gus Blake's loose talk at the Elephant had keyed Jason Kyle in to their old relationship, and at the same time to Ryder's vulnerability to a threat on the little gal. He could picture Robeson being informed at the Sunflower, ideas forming immediately as to what this new advantage meant. Pressure. Ryder forced to abandon the Kennesaw women, else birthday-gal Jenny would lose her life.

Damn Robeson. Damn Jason Kyle for a lowdown, sidewinding tale-carrier.

The list went on. Sheriff Claymore oughtn't to be in Robeson's pocket. Men like Shorty and his kid-stealing sidekick shouldn't walk the face of the earth.

But as the sun sank west into dusk, the clouds gone purple in a sky of molten brass, one fact was past denying: at the center of the mess was Ryder. He should have foreseen trouble in the saloon talk and hobbled Blake's tongue. He should not have spent time at the barbershop.

Damn!

Back off, Ryder, a voice inside commanded. *The bastard Robeson mustn't win.*

118

Someone was approaching from the opposite direction. Ryder reined in with a jerk. Along this open stretch there was no place for concealment, just treeless grassland on both sides of the road, a few isolated shrubs. So Ryder would appear as natural as a casual traveller to the oncoming horseman.

Until it was determined that the other man actually was from the Slash-Diamond-Slash. Then Ryder would go into action, and God help the feller.

Slowly, at a trot now, Ryder advanced. He had to have been seen by now, the rooster tails of dust raised by the chestnut's hoofs signals to any. Still, the other horseman came on, pace steady, a mile-eating lope. Ryder could almost make out the horseman's face, almost see the wiry buckskin's brand.

"Whoa, boy!"

Without warning, the strange rider tugged his reins, raked the buckskin with sharp rowels, and sent the horse plunging off the road and across country in a path of flight. At the same instant, a puff of gunsmoke erupted, sending hot lead screaming in Ryder's direction. The slug zinged close, too close over his head. Acting fast, the big man spurred in pursuit, and soon the chestnut was gaining.

Back on the road the flash of recognition had hit Ryder head-on. The horseman was Shorty, sometime guard of Robeson's son. One of the pair who'd snatched Jenny Blake from her mother's arms.

119

Shorty knew where the kid was. Another lead slug whined, plowed Texas soil far to the chestnut's right. Ryder jerked his own six-gun, eared the hammer. Killing Shorty was no answer, but he needed to stop the pint-size bastard. Ask polite questions. Beat the shit out of the Robeson man till he talked. Slung low over the buckskin's neck, Shorty twisted, leveled his weapon, triggered. The chestnut screamed, jolted, veered. Hit, by God! The animal leaned over, and fell. Ryder grabbed his rifle, had it unbooted as he leaped clear. He landed on his butt in deep grass, overending, rolling to a stop. Up in a split second. Jacked the Winchester's action. Aimed.

The front sight of the rifle tracked the wiry buckskin. But killing a horse! Maybe he needn't. Ryder was a marksman, a fine one, and more accurate than fast. He raised his gunsight, led shorty like a pigeon. Squeezed. A red blossom appeared on Shorty's shirt, high, shoulderblade level, and the runt threw up his arms. Toppled. Out of the saddle into mid-air, then slammed earth heavily. Ryder, up and running, covered the distance quickly coming up on the squirming ranchhand as he cocked his Colt.

Ryder kicked, and the six-gun went flying. "You big son of a bitch!"

"Easy, Shorty." The big man knelt, laid his rifle on the ground. But Shorty wasn't done yet. He launched out with a booted foot, caught Ryder on his thigh just below the balls. The big man rolled with the impact, bunched a fist, and sent it slamming into the snarling face. Now Shorty's small, hooked nose was bent over, blood pumping from it, staining his shirt.

"Where's the gal?" Ryder's voice was grave.

"What gal?"

Another blow took the little man, this one beside the ear. Ryder's advantage had to be fifty pounds. "I got to tell you who I mean, runt, I do it with knuckles." He drew back his arm.

"Wait! Wait!" The small features collapsed in fear, all execpt the fleshy, slack mouth. "Awright, the li'l Blake gal. What about her?"

Ryder said nothing. But he let his hand drift toward the handle of the sabre.

"No! Don't butcher me with that thing! Getting shot's bad enough! So me'n Cord snatched the gal. Mr. Robeson ordered it. You was supposed to chickenshit out, Ryder, leave them Kennesaw bitches on their own."

"Like I figured. What else? Is Jenny at the ranch?"

"What ranch?: The Slash-Diamond-Slash? Naw. Robeson don't want his little Billy getting wind of this."

"Billy, that's the son?"

"C'rect. Kid's got a mind of his own, loves birds, animals, y'know? Any unkindness pulled on the spread, Billy'll raise hell. Not that he's got much say-so, mind you."

Ryder wasn't being put off. "Where is she, then? You know I want Jenny Blake. Where'd you and your *compadre* hide her out, if not at Robeson's?"

"I-I—" Shorty's head slumped forward, dropping the chin on the crimson-stained shirt. There

121

was no canteen to splash the small man's face, damn it, unless his own horse carried one. Ryder glanced up, saw the buckskin standing some yards off.

At that moment, Shorty bucked violently under Ryder's hands, dove for the shell-belt at his waist and the sabre handle. He got the weapon into his fist, drawn and arcing upward with amazing speed. Ryder pitched sidelong, the filed-down blade in its razor-sharpness slitting his shirtsleeve from elbow to cuff. "Sidewinder!" The small man lifted and stabbed out again. Rolling, Ryder pulled the glittering Smith & Wesson. "Shorty! Hold it!"

Eyes pinpointing hate, the runt lunged. Ryder fired from his back, the six-gun bucking. The lead slug blasted into Shorty's cheek, and the face caved like a punctured coffee sack. His whole body followed suit, twitching once, then stretched motionless on the ground.

Shorty lay dead, face pressed to prairie sod. Ryder retrieved his sword-Bowie from the corpse's grip and sighed.

"You could've told me where to look, but you didn't, damn you. But I got me another idea. I thank you for that."

The Slash-Diamond-Slash buckskin was easy to catch. All his weapons back in place, Ryder mounted.

He rode wide around the dead chestnut, made for Robeson's through the fast-deepening dusk.

When he reined up, night had settled in completely. Good. He'd be needing the dark. The only problem was the moon, but that wouldn't rise for several hours. Dropping from the saddle, he picketed the bronc. The dry ravine he was in ran to Robeson's spread. He carried his own Winchester, left Shorty's in its boot for later. Ghosting down the gully was fairly easy. He emerged with the ranch buildings in view.

On his left. He paused a moment, refreshing memory as to the spread's whole layout. Two barns, bunkhouse, smokehouse, smithy, cookshack, a clutch of tool and supply sheds. Pole corral, a big one. The immense main house. Robeson lived in luxury befitting his image. The place had two stories in the middle, was flanked by wings tacked to either side. Directly in front wide stairs descended, but there must be more doors around to the rear. The house was Ryder's main target.

There was plenty of activity at this early hour. The cookshack, bunkhouse and area between were ablaze with lights. Punchers strolled in and out of both buildings, some carrying plates of grub, others empty-handed. From somewhere a strummed guitar joined a mouth organ in a sad tune. Well, this outfit hadn't discovered yet what 'sad' really meant. Ryder hunkered down in the grass, idly chewed a matchstick and waited. One thing he knew, it was a working spread, which meant they hit the saddle early and rode long days. Those boys down there would be hitting their blankets soon now.

When it was good and dark and quiet, he'd make his move.

The bunkhouse lamps had been out for an hour, Ryder judged from the swing of the stars, and those over in the main house just a little less. Time to move. Hoisting his rifle into his arm-crooks as he lay, the big man started to crawl, a slow way across the distance he had to cross, but undeniably the safest. The plan he'd contrived while waiting called for an approach from behind, avoiding contact with anyone, entering the house by any back way available, door or window. What room he needed, he didn't know yet, only that it must be upstairs. Bedrooms were always upstairs in rich men's dwellings. Seemed somehow to please the bastards.

The moon was up and getting high, though it was shrouded with drifting clouds. Still, he had to be careful. A hundred yards separated the swale he stood in from his destination, and he figured to cross it at a dead run. No trees, or shrubs meant no concealment, so when the moon got extra dim he readied himself. Now!

Ryder powered into motion, long legs pumping. He sprinted easily on the level ground and in a few seconds pulled up short, at a low fence surrounding a garden plot. Beyond loomed the house, just one window lit—downstairs, north wing. He crossed the garden in three strides, stepped over the fence and was at the back steps.

"What the hell! Who's that?" The shout came from behind. Ryder spun. A cowhand, lost in shadow, pissed a glittering stream into the moon's bright beams.

No time to lose! "Just me," Ryder answered.

124

"Who're you?"

His mind raced: "Cord."

"Cord's at the line shack. Hey, ain't you . . . ?" He slapped leather without tucking his member and came up fast with a long-barreled Walker Colt. Got a shot off. Blasted the door jamb by Ryder's ear. At the same time splinters were peppering Ryder's cheek he levelled the Winchester, and triggered. The blast echoed loud in the night. There went secrecy. Ryder's well-aimed slug took the puncher in the chest. The man puked black blood, then dropped dead.

Inside the house, footsteps stampeded. Ryder leaped down the steps, hugged the wall, running. Shadow spelled safety, as much safety as could be had. Now a lamp came on, and another, flooding windows with golden glow. A bright rectangle spread the ground ahead; he sped across it, dodging.

"Hey!"

"What's up?"

"A feller! There he goes!" The mighty roar of a big Sharps fifty rent the night, but Ryder, rounding the corner, only felt a slight tug at his shirt. There was pitch-black darkness, here away from the moon. He slammed an obstacle, went down, rifle flying from his hand. Men were pounding from the bunkhouse venting shouts, whistles, curses. Silhouettes appeared at the building corner. Bursts of flame spit from guns.

It was the cellar door Ryder had tripped over. He managed to haul the panel up and dive just as riddling slugs pierced the brim of the black hat.

Safe for now, he breathed to himself, *but for how long*? Damn the dark! His vest produced a lucifer and he struck it on his jeans seat. The light revealed tubs of potatoes, coiled ropes, canned goods. A sack of dried beans, a sack of rice.

A set of stairs! Ryder crossed to it, climbed to the top. Around the door showed light, the kitchen, likely, and from through the panel came the sound of voices. Men. At least three, plus a woman who spoke Spanish.

"Consuela, get lost!" Womanly steps shuffled into distance, and were heard no more. "Bert, get your ass over to the window. You see a stranger, blast 'im with that Greener."

"Right!"

"Dutch, follow me to the parlor. Ought to be somebody stationed in there."

Stomping boots receded. Ryder considered. Beyond the door was an armed-to-the-teeth guard who must be handled.

He eased the short sword from its sheath.

The door swung soundlessly inward on oil-slathered hinges. Ryder's foe was in the center of the room, facing the other way, shotgun on a table.

"Say!"

The man turned. He was burly, muscle-slabbed but slow. Ryder reached him in a flash, put the short sword at his throat. "Hush!"

"Hush, hell!" Bert was real slow-witted. The fool grabbed for the ten-gauge, opened his mouth wide to shout. Instead, his mouth emitted gurglings. With a quick stroke of the sabre Ryder had slashed the man's throat.

126

It was that or be trapped.

And Ryder trapped meant the end of little Jenny. The end of the Kennesaw widows. The triumph of Richard Robeson, would-be king of the range. As it was, Robeson's hired shootist slumped, slid along the edge of the table to its end, crashed to the bloody floor. Ryder avoided the spreading red pool as he strode for the hall.

The hall was a showplace, rigged to fit a man with lots of money and the need to display the fact. From the ceiling hung an elaborate crystal chandelier, now unlit, and on one wall a scenic painting and a large French pier mirror. Opposite, broad stairs curved upward grandly. An indigo-blue carpet underfoot masked Ryder's tread as, hand on the newel post, he round it and started up.

"By God, Hank! Look there in the mirror!"

Ryder jerked his six-gun, heard Hank's gun boom and triggered his own weapon. The man at the foot of the stair caught lead, spun, fired again, only ceilingward this time. The chandelier exploded in a rain of knifing crystal fragments and he went down shrieking.

"Dutch?" The last house guard left. "Damn it, feller, you done for Dutch!" This one was thin and tall, with a long horse face furred with mouse-brown stubble. The gun he brandished entering the hall was an Army Remington. Ryder, half-way up the long flight of stairs, crouched and fired down. Hank clutched his chest and howled as a slug from the Smith & Wesson tore through sinew and lung tissue. His gaping mouth welled blood. Before the man even had time to topple, Ryder had turned and

127

was pumping upward.

Soon now, very soon. Robeson would have heard the ruckus. More gunplay ahead? Maybe not.

He came on young Billy Robeson leaving his room. The kid was half-dressed, wearing only a shirt and a pair of britches. No shoes. No socks. No gun. "You're coming with me, kid!"

"Why?"

"I said so's why. Where's your pa?"

"In town. We going to see him?"

"Reckon not." Ryder grabbed the toothpick arm, yanked the boy. He yanked again and the kid came along. "There's got to be a back way down. Where?"

"There." Billy Robeson pointed. They took the narrow creaking staircase to the first floor, found a window for Ryder to force open. They dropped to the ground together, arms linked. The yard was crawling with men, afoot and on horseback, clothed and half-naked. All of them had guns, though. The word was out.

"Hey, you men!" Ryder shouted.

All over the yard heads swiveled. "Huh?"

"What the—?"

"Over there's the bastard!"

"Shoot to kill!"

The last to speak was a man Ryder knew from the Elephant, Burl. "No, boys! Hold your fire! Feller's got Billy!"

Ryder moved from the house wall, showing Billy prisoned in a grip of iron. The kid in front of him, he started slowly across the yard. "You know me?" he shouted.

128

"We know ya, Ryder!"

"Tell your boss I got the boy! He'll be mad, but he'll know what he's got to do!"

Burl called again across the widening distance. "Takin' the kid? Ya can't!"

"See if I can!" Ryder and the boy topped a roll of high ground, stepped backward, down and out of view. Still holding the kid, Ryder hurried to the waiting buckskin.

"Shorty's bronc!"

"He'll carry double."

When they were in the saddle, Ryder gave sharp spur.

In an hour, they were at the Rocking K. Seeing the house dark but the barn lit, Ryder reined toward the bigger structure. The buckskin trotted up to the door and halted.

Liz emerged carrying a lantern. "The Blakes, Shea, Cathy, even Jessica, they're all in bed. But I couldn't sleep, thought I might walk over, check the horses."

The lantern was held high, throwing light over both woman and the newcomers. Smoky-green eyes, wide mouth, the perky breasts under a too-tight shirt: Liz Kennesaw, flame-haired beauty. Ryder grinned at her. "Howdy, Liz."

"What's going on, Ryder? Who's that you've brought with you?"

From the saddle Billy Robeson peered down, puzzled.

"Ma?"

CHAPTER 12

Billy repeated what he'd just said. Ryder, holding him in the saddle, felt the kid squirm, was forced to tighten his grip. At the same time the big man's eyes raked Liz.

"Oh, my God! Dear God, no!" The woman's face was pale as a sheet, the mouth tight now and drawn back in a grimace from the fine, white teeth. Her upraised hand holding the lantern had started to shake.

"What the hell—" Ryder began, then stopped himself when Liz Kennesaw put down the lantern and turned to run. She ran up to the barn and inside through the open doors, disappearing. Ryder turned to Billy, "Why'd you call that lady 'Ma'?"

The kid looked scared and confused, and his voice confirmed the impression. He spoke haltingly. "Because she . . . I thought . . . I mean, it's been years and years since I was real little, but—" He started to struggle again, trying to climb down off the horse. "Aw, shucks, I remember my ma's hair!"

The Rocking K premises had sprung into life. A

lamp came on in the bunkhouse, a couple of bright windows suddenly poured yellow illumination from the house. Across the yard Terry Shea could be seen coming on the run, hitching suspenders over his scrawny shoulders, stuffing in shirttails. "Ryder!"

From the other direction came, "What's up? We heard. . ." Shea had pounded up to the standing buckskin and Gus and Sarah Blake were right at his heels. Cathy and Jessica, wearing flimsy night-gowns, could be seen jumping from the veranda.

"Shea," Ryder snapped. "You know this kid!" It was a statement, not a question.

The former swamper's mouth gaped. "Christ, it's Robeson's boy! How'd you get hold of the li'l devil?"

The big man slipped from the saddle, still hold-ing the kid pinned to him. "A snatch. Figured to make a swap for Jenny Blake, a way to make old Robeson back off. Now I ain't so sure." He thrust Billy at Shea. "Watch him. Don't let him get away. Tell the others I'm going in to talk to Liz."

"Sure, Ryder, only. . ."

Terry Shea was left holding Billy's arm, watch-ing Ryder's back as he strode for the barn after Liz.

Entering, he scanned the bright area within the doors. Nobody in sight. Damn! He widened his search, stalking back past the stall where the lame bay stood flicking its tail, crossed the spot where he'd once lain spreadeagled. "Liz! Damn it, Liz!" he shouted. No response. Only then did he hear the faint sniffling from farther back, coupled with an occasional sob.

He came to the last stall in the row.

"Here you are."

She looked up from where she sat, backed to the stall's wall. The great eyes were swimming. The woman's flame-red hair carried bits of straw, the shirt's loose buttons showed a pale flash of breast. But Liz Kennesaw was beyond care for her appearance. "Ryder, is that you? What do you want?"

He wouldn't fool with her, not now. "Information."

"Go away."

"You know I won't."

"Well, then!" She crossed her legs under her and sat up straighter, Indian style. "There. At least now my tears can run down my face. I have to guess, mister, you like to watch pain."

"Better than causing pain. And that's exactly what I just came back from doing. Over to the Slash-Diamond-Slash tonight, there was killing, and a lot of it. Too much, I'm thinking now. Of course, Robeson shouldn't have tried to get at me by kidnapping Blake's kid, involve those innocent folks in a fracas. He's got to hate you, Liz, plenty."

Liz Kennesaw snorted. "You're exactly on target, Ryder."

"Want to spill the story?"

"It's a long one."

"Then I reckon I'll just set."

They sat face to face backed to the stall walls in the stuffy, dark corner of the barn. Ryder could just about make out the woman's face.

"Truth?" she asked.

"Truth."

"Then, truth you'll have, by Jesus!"

He couldn't tell if Liz was cursing or promising. Maybe some of both. He waited silently for her to begin the yarn as to why Robeson's kid had called her "Ma".

"It all started ten years ago, come fall. I was sixteen, a Kansas farm-girl born of Bible-thumpers, grown up on a homestead silly and bored. There were a few cows and a few crops, and I milked cows while the crops failed. Every year the crops failed. Well, one day a passing stranger stopped his horse and dropped in. A well-dressed man who flashed money, so my pa, broke as usual, let him board a few nights in our soddy. That's how I met Richard."

"Robeson." Ryder idly fished a matchstick.

"Robeson, yes. To make a long story short, I fell for Richard, and when he was leaving I packed my poke. That morning instead of being at my chores I was on the trail, run off with a man twice my age I'd known three days. But I never looked back. Robeson took me to his ranch up in Dakota Territory, and I was soon expecting. Billy was delivered by a squaw in the middle of winter, and in the spring Richard went off to the war." Liz smiled faintly. "Jess says you fought for the South, Ryder. Richard was Yankee."

"Officer?"

"Infantry colonel."

Ryder shrugged. The birch flavor of his lucifer was dead. He snapped the stick and tossed it.

Liz didn't go on right away. He waited.

"Here's the hard part coming up, Ryder."

"Take your time."

She did. At least five more minutes dragged along in the silent gloom. "Richard came home from the War Between the States changed. I'd waited for him, of course, on the ranch he'd left in the care of Indian employees. But Richard had been wounded, and wasn't a whole man like before. It turned him mean and bitter."

"You couldn't take it?" Ryder queried in the half-dark.

"I couldn't take it. Oh, he seemed normal outwardly, to others. To little Billy whom he truly loved. Richard's love of that boy took over his whole life. So for the second time in my life I ran off, I left my son behind."

"The kid was what—six?"

She nodded.

"Big enough so's he could remember you. He remembered you tonght."

Liz Kennesaw tossed her red hair. "I'm not proud of leaving my son. But Richard was rich. He loved the lad. But he started to hate me and. . ." she didn't finish.

"You needed a new life. You found it here in Texas with Joe Kennesaw. Robeson traced you, though. He wanted you back. But you were married to Joe."

"Richard and I never married."

"Hey, in there! You two all right?" It was Gus Blake's voice cutting the heavy barn air. Heavy boots tromped the hardwood floor.

"We're all right!" Ryder called. He turned to

135

Liz. "Guess the folks have got plumb worried. We better go."

Liz nodded reluctantly.

"We'll be right out, Gus! Go on up to the house, we'll be right there for coffee!" Ryder yelled.

"Sarah's made some! We'll be seein" you." The footsteps went away.

"Let's go, gal," Ryder said.

They were on the veranda with mugs of Blake's Special Brew. Ryder, his scuffed, worn army boots propped on the railing, looked across at the woman in the porch swing. "Liz, I got to ask another thing."

"Do it." The redhead eyed him over her steaming mug.

"Robeson's got some things on his side. He's a sick-in-the-head son of a bitch, but he wants this ranch, and he wants you, too."

"I know. He told me when he first came to Texas."

"But the others never knew. You never let on." She didn't answer. "Liz, you could be to blame for Joe's death, in a way. Jack's and Jamie's too. You didn't warn them."

"How could I? There was the shame. A child out of wedlock."

"Oughtn't to cost lives. So many lives. You're hanging on at the Rocking K now. Why?"

"Richard's not going to win. He can have his boy, I got used to the loss of Billy years ago. That is, he can have his boy if he'll swap Jenny for him. But he can't have me! Me or this ranch! The

136

Rocking K's ours, mine and my sisters'-in-law!"

"I see." A rosy sunrise was painting the east. They'd talked the night away. Breakfast pans were clattering inside the house. Ryder's last meal had been noon yesterday. His stomach was raising hell. "Reckon you want me to keep your secret."

She nodded.

"I will. But Liz, when I promised to help you and Cathy and Jessica, I didn't know everything."

She stared at the sunrise. "If you want to light out, I can't stop it."

"I don't go back on promises," Ryder said. "I'll go on battling Robeson for you gals. Only, without killing from now on. Here's the notion I got—"

All at once Terry Shea was in the yard, running, skipping, waving his brand-new Texas-creased hat. His face carried a grin.

"A rider. Spotted him from back there! One feller, and he's got little Jenny in the saddle with him! Fixing to swap, that's it, for sure! Robeson wants his Billy, by God!"

Ryder smiled too. "Put the kid up on Shorty's buckskin. Let him go home in style."

"Goddamnit, I told you to get that shit shoveled before lunchtime!"

"I know, but—"

"No ifs, ands, or buts, goddamnit! When I say 'jump,' feller, you're gonna jump, do you unnerstand?"

Gus Blake leaned his pitchfork against the wall, grunted, reached toward his hip pocket where resided a damp bandana. His flat slab of a face ran sweat in rivers, the shirt on his back was soaked clear through. Outside the sun was blazing high noon, and no breeze stirred to cut the searing heat. Inside the barn, pure hell reigned. It was an oven. His wife had volunteered for dinner fixing. He trusted the Kennesaw women weren't giving her the same hard time their son-of-a-bitch segundo was dishing him.

"Blast you, move!" Terry Shea barked. Being the boss rather than the worker enabled him to appear the fashion plate. Unwrinkled trousers, store-stiff shirt damp only at the armpits. A new tooled gunbelt supporting a holster with a new Frontier Colt, and a cream-colored, wide-brimmed, high-crowned Stetson. Even a Lone-Star belt buckle.

"You gonna move your ass?"

"Listen, Shea—"

"Hold it!" Shea held up his hand. To make his point required concentration, and being cold sober felt so strange. "Gus Blake, do you or don't you work now for the Rocking K? Signed on after Ryder got your daughter back, him bein' in a bind?"

"Hell, I do. He couldn't hire him any hands in town, and it seemed I owed him."

"Do or don't you live here on the spread now, your wife Sarah, too, plus the little gal?"

"Do."

"Havin' give up the saloon trade, which your wife hates anyhow."

"By God, it is true, all of it. But so what, Shea? You got a point?"

Terry swept off the hat and became a foot shorter. Stood in the middle of the barn floor fingering the soft, smooth felt as he tried to get his thoughts together.

"I got hired first!" he said. "That puts me into givin' you orders for a change, Gus Blake! At the Elephant, *you* bossed *me* ! And were powerful hard too goddamn often!"

"Damn it, Terry, you was nigh always fallin'-down drunk! You needed me to ride you."

"I ain't drunk no more! I swore to Ryder when I come here, no more hooch! Hooch cost me my Slash-Diamond-Slash job, and I learned me my lesson." Shea drew up tall, all five-foot-four inches of him. "So, Blake, *since* I'm sober, and *since* I'm in charge here, *you* get *your* ass to shoveling that horseshit."

"Shea, better watch the cussing. Lots of women-folk on this spread," Ryder said from the doorway. He strode in and straight back to the lame bay gelding's stall, pulled the gate wide. "Yo, boy, how's the leg?" The horse knew its master, tossed its head and mane.

"Ryder, I was only—"

"The bronc could use exercise. Might fit into my plans." The big man looked at Shea, and couldn't help breaking into a broad grin. "How's it going, Terry?"

"Er, good, I reckon."

"Fine. Gus, your little Jenny has been asking after you at the house. You don't smell too bad. Why not take a rest, run on over there?"

Gus Blake flicked a look at Shea.

139

"It's all right," Ryder assured him. "I got to talk a spell here to Terry. Before I head for town."

When Gus Blake had stashed his fork, mopped his face, and was hotfooting toward his little girl, Ryder motioned to Shea to join him on the nearest hay bale. The ex-swamper hitched his gunbelt, snapped his suspenders, and eased down beside the big man.

"Shea, you've been doing right well. A whole day on the spread and you've not touched liquor."

Shea shrugged, but his face became wreathed in smile wrinkles.

"You like it here at the Rocking K?"

An assenting nod.

"And I reckon it's like sugar on the cherry cobbler, the fact you get to boss around your old boss, Blake."

Terry couldn't keep from grinning, at the same time slapping his knee with his Stetson. "I'm glad for the chance you give me, Ryder. And o'course, thanks too to Miz Liz, Miz Jessica and Miz Cathy. All fine women, I'm learning, the salt of the earth. A lot of gumption, never mind bein' widows."

"But they need our help, Shea and a lot of it. Robeson's swap of little Jenny for his Billy boy means no more than that we outfoxed the bastard once. He'll sure as hell be trying new mischief as soon as he can, try to force the Kennesaw women out."

"So?" Terry Shea said, scratching his bumpy nose.

"So, that's where you come in. You worked for Robeson once. You not only know the Slash-

140

Diamond-Slash from line to line, you know the men. I'm going to be tangling with the jaspers, I want their weak spots. You can tell me."

Shea frowned. "I dunno."

"Don't know if you're willing to help that way?"

"Aw, hell, no! I'll tell what you want. I just don't see how it'll help."

"Just let me handle it." Ryder fished a lucifer match, set it in his teeth. "Look, last night I killed fellers calling each other Hank, Bert, Dutch. There was another, I didn't hear his name. Hooknose jasper with oversized ears."

"Selby Gaines, by God! A mean son of a bitch! No loss to the world!"

"Of Robeson's bunch—not plain cow wranglers but the fighters—who's left best?"

"Shit!" Shea didn't hesitate, but rattled off six names as fast as his tongue would go. "Pike Cady, Luke Cord. Burl Anderson, feller name of Hotchkiss. Sep Turnbull. And o'course, Gato Mendez. Mendez is the worst."

"A Mexican?"

"Breed. A bad one. Good with guns and fists and toadstabbers. He carries two blades, a broad and a narrow."

Ryder scrubbed a jaw with a palm, said nothing.

"You take out that crew, it leaves plain punchers, only. Rope men. Nut-cutters. Them that's handy with brandin' irons. But, Christ, to take on them six with guns, even you, Ryder." Shea shook his head.

"Likely won't come to that."

Terry Shea gaped. "Huh?"

"Look, I'm riding into town. I want you to keep these for me." The big man was loosening the weapons belt with the sheathed six-gun and sword-Bowie. "My rifle, too." Behind him, his saddle rode a stall gate. He unbooted the Winchester and passed it to the older man.

"Into town bare-handed? By God, man."

Ryder declared, "It's best. I learned some things this morning about this little range war, and who's really to blame. I want no more killing if it can be helped. Now, you going to tell me what those tough boys look like?"

As Terry Shea did so, Ryder tossed his saddle on the bay. He cinched up, tightened the bridle and bit carefully, and led the animal out into bright day.

The big man swung up, reined the horse around and spurred for Yorktown.

There was only one thing to say, and Shea said it.

"Well, I'll be damned!"

CHAPTER 13

Ryder reined in and dismounted in front of Yorktown's one and only livery stable. Snubbing the bay to the hitch rail, he took a long minute to eye the men and women drifting from one to another of the shops making up the seedy, false-fronted row. Brown's Mercantile seemed to have won the bulk of the button, bow and ribbon trade as females, young and old, fat and thin, swarmed thick as comb bees around the broom-propped door. Next to the general store lay the boarded-up Elephant, where there was no action at all. The town's liquor business, Ryder guessed, had moved across to the Palace. The big man turned up the boardwalk in that direction.

"Ryder, wait! Want a word with ya!"

The big man paused, and out of the corner of an eye glimpsed a form through the window of the sheriff's office. Bat Claymore was up and on his legs, between desk and door. As he stepped out, Ryder noted, the tin star gleamed on the lawman's shirt as if freshly polished. Well, better to spend a morning plying a soft rag than hunting drifters and road agents. Killers and kid stealers.

"Ryder!" The lawman wheezed up to the big man, the cannonball belly under the star lifting and falling with the exertion. "I scouted me some fellers for a posse to go after little Jenny Blake," Claymore offered. "Way I figure it, we—"

Ryder snorted. "Can't make yourself look good with that three-ring circus you're planning, sheriff. The gal's been found, and is with her ma this minute, the pair happy as fawns."

"Huh? Where?"

"Never mind the Blake family's whereabouts now, Claymore. But I might mention where the key to the kid was. Would you believe, the Slash-Diamond-Slash?"

"Huh? Damn if Robeson didn't say something."

The fat man's tongue was no good with words. Ryder swung his wide shoulders sidelong, tried to brush past the sheriff and be on his way. Bulk won out, though, and he was blocked. "Lose your shootin' iron, Ryder? Don't see that short sword thing you allus wear, neither."

"Look, Claymore—"

"You're in Yorktown now, mister." The pig eyes narrowed down even more than usual. "Now, if'n you go get hurt on account you can't defend yourself, don't come whinin' around afterwards."

"Sheriff, most lawmen in the country would welcome folks to tote fewer weapons. They'd be glad as hell, a feller sees fit to go light in their town."

"Not in Yorktown." Claymore took a step back so as to be half in, half out of the jailhouse doorway. "I allus say, a real man takes care of himself." He pulled his head in quickly and vanished.

Ryder shrugged, wiped his face on his sleeve. Hotter than ever. What he needed was a cool beer.

The Palace had a piano, but no musician. The chesty, flounce-skirted woman occupying the stool was playing "Yellow Rose" with all the skill of a Piute medicine man. Ryder steeled himself, and made his way to the battered teak bar, full of scratches and bulletholes. No one seemed to mind as they bellied up, planted feet on the tarnished brass rail. A barman with head bald as a cue-ball ambled over, wiped plump hands on a dingy apron.

"What'll it be?"

"Is the beer cold?"

"This kinda weather? Hell, our ice-house went warm last month, fresh out of river ice. Got some bottles of Busch here, though. Don't taste too bad warm."

Ryder laid down a shiny nickle. "Sold, feller."

The place was crowded, the whole rear half of the room given over to gambling. A tinhorn monte-thrower plied his trade. A busy faro layout flanked him. Ryder swigged Busch as he let his eyes find and come to rest on the poker table. Familiar faces surrounded it: Sander Billings, Horace Poole, Jason Kyle— Robeson's extra ear. But more of interest was a giant of a man seated in the next chair: bull-necked, red-faced, scarred from chin to ear. The scar ran the jawline, a jagged band of white.

From Terry Shea's description, Ryder was ready

to bet it was Luke Cord. He edged closer to the table, cocked his ears.

Horace Poole, gray beard wagging, tossed his hand in to the center of the table. "Fold," he croaked in his brittle voice. "And count me outa the game, by God. Nigh supper time."

"Supper? This time o' day?"

"Actually m'wife's t'tea at her sister's. Injun maid's home alone, cleanin' up."

Everybody laughed but Kyle and Cord. Cord, one of the hardcases who'd kidnapped little Jenny, didn't look able to laugh. Poole shoved his chair back from the green table, got up stiffly. Scooped his stake money into his hat. Shambled off.

"Anyone call?" Jason Kyle said. Nobody did, and with face absolutely expressionless, Kyle raked in the pot.

Ryder had moved in to palaver. He loudly cleared his throat, grasped the back of the empty chair. "Got room it appears, gents. Mind if I sit in?" Sander Billings threw him a welcoming expression. Kyle frowned. The others shrugged.

"Anybody can play." Cord's voice was hoarse, a hinge needing oil. He stared with yellow eyes. "That is, if he's got the money."

"I got the money." Ryder showed a roll of bills. When nobody objected, he sat down in the battered ladder-back, dropped the money on the green baize tabletop. "Draw poker?"

"What you seen, weren't it?"

Ryder was good at draw poker. The game held more challenge of skill than stud.

"Table stakes," Jason Kyle said with measured

politeness.

"Fair enough."

The deck was passed for Luke Cord to deal.

A half-hour of play was enough, Ryder decided early. As the cards were shuffled and dealt, and the money changed hands, he kept a sharp eye on the saloon-wall banjo clock. He'd been alternating winning and losing a series of small pots, playing close to his highpocketed leather vest. He concentrated extra hard on hands when he noticed Cord plunging heavily. Not just any opportunity would do.

"Call, by God!"

"Shit!"

"Aces full, mister." The pot was raked in by the fellow sitting next to Billings, a drummer in a cheap suit. The former ranch-owner merely cocked his derby forward and smiled. He'd folded and was safe. Ryder shrugged and Jason Kyle merely sat wordless. Luke Cord was the big loser, both for the hand and evening. Ryder had watched the scarface's stake slipping for thirty minutes. Now only a few greenbacks and half-eagle coins littered the green baize in front of the giant.

Ryder's deal. The deck was passed to him.

Ryder shuffled slowly, conscious of the pairs of eyes focused on him. The squinting gaze of Cord could almost be felt. He offered the cut. Sander Billings rapped the deck. Cord's frown deepened, but Ryder was already passing out the cards.

The drummer opened with a dollar. Jason Kyle stayed, as did, after a brief pause, Luke Cord.

147

Billings, nursing a grin, tossed his cards down. Ryder held the heart ace, paired treys, and a couple of garbage cards. Bluff time. He raised a buck.

Everybody stayed, but Cord didn't appear happy. "Gimme three." Ryder did so, then dealt himself two, replacing discards. Kyle and the drummer dropped out, leaving Ryder and the scarface. Luke Cord grinned wickedly, tossed a gold coin in the pot.

"A half-eagle, mister. Gonna cost you to see."

"Half-eagle, and here's another." The big man stroked his mustache, depleted his pile by the heavy gold coin. Meantime, Luke Cord was fingering his stake.

Ryder had missed his ace but drawn a second pair: treys and eights. A shit-ass hand. Still, having kept three, he'd apparently baffled his adversary. Veins stood out on Cord's low forehead, the scar on his chin had turned bright pink.

"You're bluffin', mister."

"If you say so."

"Awright, here." The pot grew twenty dollars as the giant tossed a gold piece. Ryder matched it.

"Plus another," Ryder offered.

"Shit!" Cord was counting out bills. "Eighteen, nineteen . . . I'm short. Take a marker?"

Ryder glanced right, left. Gray eyes holding on Cord. "Afraid not."

The red face grew redder. "Hell, a dollar's all I'm short."

"I can count, feller. Put up or shut up."

Safely out of the action, the drummer leaned

back in his seat and grinned. Sander Billings, too, seemed to be enjoying himself. Jason Kyle was a poker-faced Comanche.

"You gonna pull this shit? I got a winnin' hand."

"No put up, no see." Ryder waited a long minute. Cord just sat. "Well." Ryder raked in the pot.

"Wait a goddamned minute!" Quick as a rattler's strike, Luke Cord's hand shot out. Flipped Ryder's cards over. "Two lousy pair? I had kings full!"

"Luck of the draw. Gents," Ryder said, turning to the others, "I'm afraid that's about all the time I can spare this afternoon. Reckon I'll bow out."

"What?" Luke Cord's massive shoulders shook. He was building up a head of rage.

"I believe you heard it, feller. Now, if you'll just let me pass."

"You gonna bluff and run? Leave me high and dry? That stinks, mister, you know that? Stinks worse'n burro shit!"

"You lost fair and square."

"Damn you."

Ryder's voice held a deadly calm. "Cord, let me past."

"You know m'name! Stinks of a set-up, by God! Damn if you're gonna get away with this!" With a mighty heave, Cord plucked the table from the floor, sent it flying. The other cardplayers leaped from its path. All over the saloon heads turned, and there was a scramble as men vacated the area to Ryder's rear.

"Draw!" Luke yelled, as his hamlike hand shot

holster ward, then poised as his mouth fell open.
"You ain't packin' no hogleg!"

Ryder stood, quiet.

"By God! Damn! Chickenshit bastard knows I
won't shoot an unarmed jasper. Hell, I'll whop 'im
with my paws! Here!" He whipped the gunbelt
from his waist, thrust it into the hands of Kyle.
Then in a clumsy but powerful move, he launched
a blow with an arm like a tree.

"Fight!" a man at the bar whooped.

"Christ! Look out!"

The bystanders' yells didn't faze Ryder. The big
man dodged, and Cord's fist sliced air. Glancing
right, left, he took in the Palace, noted bar drinkers lined and watching, elbows digging ribs, rows
of smiling teeth. Closer by, the gambling crowd
had spread out, no longer fearing gunplay. Now a
ring was formed around the combatants. Ryder
heard bets being placed.

"Gimme Cord, two to one."

"Fifty on Luke, feller!"

"Luke Cord!"

Ryder wasn't the favorite.

"Play with me, hey?" Cord was snarling.

Then he charged again, this time more swift,
more cagey, to catch Ryder with a body blow, and
send him backpedaling. Ryder moved forward
now, fists doubled, feinted a hook, feinted a jab,
both times pulling back at the last instant. Cord
wasn't fast, but had tremendous arms—muscles so
packed they nearly split his shirt. Hands like
sledges. A great bull neck sloping into huge shoulders.

150

But Ryder's own shoulders were just as wide. He dropped the right one, levelled a punch at the giant's jaw, connecting. Luke Cord went careening back. Cord slammed through the row of spectators, fetched up hard against the wall, roaring.

The whole Palace shook. Cord came off the wall, kicked a chair, shattering it, and charged again. A glancing swipe caught Ryder's temple. Ryder blinked, pain lancing, and for a split second saw the lamps go out. A blob of blackness crawled up through his brain, tried to hold on. Then he shook himself. The bear of a man swam back into focus. Ryder launched a blow to the gut, with all his strength.

Cord hinged over, took one stumbling step, and fell against Ryder. Wrapped him in a hug.

The voices of the bettors yelled, "Ten on Cord, dammit. Odds five to one now!"

"Done!"

"I'll take the stranger, by God!"

"Hit the bastard, hit 'im!"

Ryder heard it all through ears gone deadish, but still vaguely sensed that most of the gents standing around backed Cord. He tried to break the brutal grip, failed. Tried to knee his opponent's groin, but he was pinned too tight. Ryder found himself winded and weakening. Cord's stinking breath made him want to vomit.

Ryder drew his head back with the last of his strength, slammed it forward again to batter Cord's potato nose. The bone crunched as it yielded. The man screeched, blood gushing in a hot, red stream. Ryder's face was splashed. Solid brow met soft nose again. The giant's grip loosed, and welcome air poured in the big man's lungs. Ryder linked fingers, flexed his arms. Cord, shrugged off, stumbled away, creating an opening. Ryder twisted, dipped.

Knees flexed, he sent his fist upward in a round-house arc. Ryder's knuckles met the scar-marked jaw. Cord went hurtling.

"Hurray!" a sideliner shouted.

"I'll take Ryder!" The crowd too had begun to sense the end.

Luke Cord slammed the wall, folded over like a concertina. In another second he was stretched on the floor, unmoving. Spittle dribbled from his slack mouth.

The Palace Saloon erupted in cheers. "Helluva fight!"

"Well done, stranger."

"Drinks! I'm buyin' for the house!" Sander Billings had won heavily from his bets on Ryder. Ryder staggered over and ground his worn, black army boot into Cord's outstretched hand. The cheers from the crowd hid a sickening crunch of bone and cartilage.

Offered whisky, brandy, anything he wanted, Ryder simply declined. "Thanks just the same, gents. Kinda tired. Best be getting on." But at the batwings he paused. Jason Kyle stood at the front bar-corner. "Yeah, it's Cord's gun hand got busted. Bad, too. Bad as hell. Mister Robeson's gonna shit pink feathers."

Outside, Ryder grinned brightly at the sky. Job done.

152

At the Rocking K they had a bath waiting. In the kitchen an immense zinc tub stood filled with scalding water. When Ryder walked in, he was surrounded by women, from Cathy and Jessica to a blushing Sarah Blake. Liz wasn't around.

"What's this?"

"Surprise," Jess Kennesaw said.

"Yes, ain't it?" Cathy said.

"Ryder, w-we wanted, I mean *they* wanted, I mean—" Clearly Sarah, older, quite a bit more modest, was at a loss for words.

"Ladies, I surely thank you. But—"

"Leave you completely on your own, so's you'll get plumb clean."

"Wouldn't dream of peekin', would we?"

"Oh, no!"

"Look, Ryder, we even drew the window shades."

"Here's a towel."

"Here's the soap."

"Bye," they all called in unison.

Suddenly Ryder found himself alone. The females gone, water steamed in the tub enticingly. A chair was handy to hold soapdish, combs, cloths. Christ! Just what his bruised ribs needed!

Although Luke Cord had been the loser in the Palace, Ryder wasn't entirely unscathed. Losing no more time, he stripped off boots, vest, slightly frayed shirt. Trousers followed the rest, and he stood in balbriggans. The women had said they wouldn't peek, hadn't they? Not Sarah Blake, surely. For the others, it was hard to tell.

Hell, the water was getting cold. Ryder shed his

underwear and stood naked beside the tub.

"Excuse me! Figured you'd be needin' this," Cathy said as she walked back into the room.

Ryder jumped for the tub, sank his big frame as much as possible below the surface. The lovely blond sashayed over, held out a sponge.

"Fetched you something. Here."

"Leave it on the chair."

"I want you to take it. Don't aim to leave it where it might be out of reach."

Ryder was cramped into an almost doubled-over position, knees high under his chin, the powerful shoulders hunched. "What's wrong?" he said as he saw her pained expression.

"Scars. My God, Ryder, look at you!"

Which was exactly what the woman was doing. Down through water not yet soap-frothed, but perfectly clear. Ryder's organ stirred, grew under the bold, frank scrutiny.

"Well, I been in some fights."

"How'd you get this one?" A delicate finger traced a dimple just under his armpit.

"That? Oh, a gun showdown, much as I recollect. Up Abilene way."

"This?"

"The three-inch knife scar? Shoot, just a little ruckus over in Soccoro. Me'n a feller called Tramp. He come out of it worse."

"And this?"

"Lakota chief Bear Claw." The last wound had been low, abdominal: not deep, just showy. To have studied it, Cathy must have also noticed his state.

154

"What's goin' on?" Jessica Kennesaw crossed the kitchen and marched to tubside, arms loaded with a stack of fluffy towels.

"Ryder's showin' me his scars," Cathy explained.

"That so? Let *me* see." Jess deposited the towels on the chair seat, bent so low over Ryder that her soft breast brushed him through her dress. "Oh, my goodness! What's this, a hatchet slice?"

"An Indian named Bear Claw gave it to him. From the Lapoka tribe."

"Lakota," Ryder corrected. Now both women's eyes were focused on that part of him. Any more growth, his manhood would break surface.

"I never heard of the Lakotas. Did you Cathy?"

"No, but they got to be mean."

Ryder sighed. "They're a branch of the Sioux Nation, ladies. Now, I thank you for the sponge and towels. This here trail dust—"

"Ain't he hairy, Jess?"

"Hairy and *cute*! Why, chest's pelted like a beaver. I just got to touch it."

Her hand, outstretched, was an inch from his skin when the back door popped open. In came a strong draft of evening air, plus Liz Kennesaw, carrying a large, thick ledger.

"Oh! I didn't realize!"

The black-haired beauty and the blonde whirled to face the redhead. Both were flushed pink in their surprise, but not so top-to-toenail fire-red embarrassed as the man in the tub.

"Ryder, I've been hunting for you."

"Liz, have you, now?" The hovering lovelies

towered over him, all the time his mouth too dry to spit. "You want to scrub my back or something? Maybe count my scars?"

"Don't be crude! We've guests in the house, the Blakes. How would it look if poor, dear Sarah would happen in here, find us three with our hands all over you? Don't you answer! I'd be shamed to tears!"

Ryder subsided, both in word and body. Damn it, son of a bitch!

"Look at this." Liz plopped down on the chair, opened the ledger wide across shapely knees. From the corner of his eyes, Ryder noted Cathy's and Jess's tiptoed departure. "Ah. Here we are."

The figures thrust at Ryder meant nothing to him. He blurted, "Huh?"

"We're low on supplies. Unless the Rocking K larder is restocked, all the new people here plus we old-timers are going to starve. I want to send Terry Shea to town with the wagon.

Ryder peered up. "I'll go."

"Tomorrow."

"Count me in."

"Ryder, you were in town today. What you accomplished, I can't imagine, but you don't have to—"

"Work so hard?"

She nodded, so violently her tightly tied-back hair lost some strands to freedom.

"Liz, I'll go," the big man repeated. "I'll just take the wagon and fetch supplies. Make a list of what's needed, I'll take it in the morning. I want to go to Yorktown anyhow. I got lots to do."

A look of deep curiosity fell on Liz's face. "Lord, you *do* have a raft of scars, Ryder. Here on your shoulder . . ."

"New Mexico Territory."

"Here?"

"Tennessee. Gatlinburg, 1862."

Her lake-blue eyes probed mischievously, seemed focused with fascination below his water-line.

"That's the Lakota wound, damn it! La-ko-ta. Spent six months up to west Nebraska, these redskins started burning, raping."

"Mr. Ryder, why the subjects you bring into an innocent conversation! The idea!" With a grin she threw the washcloth at him. Before he realized, he'd raised his hands to catch it, exposing . . .

"You'll have the supplies list in the morning, early!" she assured him with a smile.

The door closed gently behind her. And he could hear Liz Kennesaw's laughter tinkling all her long way down the hall.

CHAPTER 14

The battered Studebaker wagon rolled to a halt in front of Brown's Mercantile and the driver stepped from seat to wheel to ground with long-limbed ease. Another broiling Texas day under a seething sun, the hazed, high sky painted pale and wispy with clouds. Ryder, like both the wagon and team, was caked by dust all over. The gritty red granules had even penetrated the clean shirt and jeans he'd donned after last night's bath.

After Liz had departed with her precious ledger book, he'd remained alone and undisturbed in the tub in the Rocking K kitchen. Under the circumstances, getting clean was no problem.

And, damn it, not much fun, either.

Now he hitched the belt at his waist, again unencumbered by weapons. "Horses, you got to wait. I shouldn't be gone longer than the rest of the morning." So saying, Ryder made his way into the cooler interior of the store.

A man in an apron stood at a counter, neat as a catalog illustration with his red sleeve garters and heavily pomaded hair. The merchant's wares surrounded him: everything from bolt cloth to saddles to shiny tins of peaches and fish either set on shelves or hung from wall pegs. The big man pulled out his list, thrust it into the other's soft, pale hand. Down the length of a narrow nose, through thick spectacles, the paper got read. "Yeah, I carry all this stuff," the man singsonged.

"There's a wagon out front with the Rocking K brand burned on the side. Fill the order, load it up. About how long, do you reckon?"

The townsman blinked as if sleepy, scratched his armpit. "Best allow an hour."

Ryder nodded and started to turn, remembered something important, and stepped back up to the cluttered counter. "Thought of something else. Shells. Winchester .44s. Two boxes."

"That be it?"

"That's it."

"Like I said," the merchant grunted. "Be ready in an hour." He was speaking to Ryder's back as the big man stalked out.

Once on the boardwalk and breathing fresh air Ryder paused and thought. Where to go next? The Palace? The table-busting, chair-smashing fight with Luke Cord had done little to make him popular with the barkeep. Still, if he were really bent on tangling with Slash-Diamond-Slash hands, what better spot was there?

"There! Why damn if it isn't the very bastard, by Jesus!" Ryder spun. A pair of ugly, scowling hardcase types moved in lockstep out of the wagon's shadow. "Hold it there, Ryder!"

"Gents? Your pleasure?" Ryder said politely. But the pair didn't want politeness.

160

"Told ya he'd be along," the taller hardcase rasped, sneering. "Rocking K wagon figures to have a low-down sidewinder for a driver."

"Right as rain, Pike."

"So, we got 'im where we want 'im, friend Septimus."

Pike Cady and Sep Turnbull. Two more gunsels from the army of Robeson. Ryder grinned. Even though both were big bruisers. Even though he'd encountered them together.

"You whupped a feller name of Cord yesterday in the saloon, mister." The speaker was Turnbull, tall, rawboned, his eyes cold as pebbles in their deep sockets.

"Luke, he's our good friend." Cady was squat, but thick. A muscle-slabbed barrel chest made the hardcase look topheavy. He needed a shave.

Now the pair separated, one stepping to either side of Ryder. Clawed hands hovered near six-gun butts.

"Draw on an unarmed feller?" Ryder stood with legs apart, lifted his arms to show he wore no gun.

"Bastard! Same stunt as he pulled with Lukey! Hell, though, we don't need guns to kick this son of a bitch's ass!" They unbuckled leisurely, almost as if enjoying themselves, and tossed belts and holstered Colts over their shoulders into the wagon box.

"Now!"

"Grab 'im!"

Ryder had planned to carry on the brawl in the street, passersby serving as fair-minded witnesses. But at the moment, a quick glance in both

161

directions happened to pick up nobody, not a soul, on the boardwalk. The big man was crashed into by the man called Cady, grabbed by Turnbull at the shirt collar and spun around. An opening he hadn't noticed confronted Ryder, a narrow alley running along the store's side wall.

A fist of iron hammered Ryder's gut. He jack-knifed, and while still doubled over in pain was shoved into and along the passage. At the other end, he found himself tripped up, flung headlong on hard-packed earth. Ryder's shoulder skidded; his shirt ripped. He blinked dust out of his eyes. The three men were together inside a box, a breezeless, stifling area between blank-walled buildings.

Ryder climbed to his knees. His head throbbed where it had struck ground. Standing over him were the pair. Sneering. Mocking. Cady spat brown tobacco juice into Ryder's face.

"Son of a bitching turd!"

Sep Turnbull positioned himself just right, launched a kick at the prone man's ribcage. Before it could connect Ryder rolled, twisted, kicked out himself. Cady, taken in the tender groin area, screamed, was catapulted back. Turnbull, circling, watched his chance. Ryder bounded up, crouched. "Sidewinder!" Sep Turnbull croaked out. Then the barrel-chest charged.

Ryder, timing his blow, threw a bunched fist of granite. Turnbull must have seen it coming but failed to dodge. The fist took him in the chest, stopped him cold. Veins popped on his forehead, the thick-lipped mouth fell open. Ryder hit the

162

mouth hard. Knuckles met lips, blood erupted. Ryder moved in for the kill.

He was jumped from behind. Cady's arm hooked his throat. Ryder's hat kited away, sent his dark hair flying. Soon thick fingers wrapped in the hair and yanked. Sharp pain cut into Ryder's scalp, throat, voicebox. The pressure tightened, and tightened some more. He couldn't breathe. Ryder's head was drawn back, forced to one side. Sweat rivering into stinging eyes, agonized, Ryder was helpless.

"I want 'im, Pike!" Turnbull yelled.

A form loomed in front of Ryder. The ugly, leering face of big Sep Turnbull. Then a punch to his midsection took the pinned man. Another. A wave of nausea rose in Ryder, tall as the sky, wide as four horizons. "One more, this time in the balls!"

Ryder, desperate, flung his feet out, and suspended by Cady's vicious choke hold, connected full force with the gut of Turnbull. Sep coughed, doubled, spun vomiting yellow slime on himself and the sun-baked ground. The sudden weight-shift pulled Cady off balance. Ryder fell, breaking the choke grip, and he was free.

Ryder whirled, slammed knuckles to the lantern jaw. Cady flew back, arms windmilling. A left cross buried into his gut sent the hardcase to one knee. And another blow, and another! The man went down in a heap, twitching.

Turnbull, grizzly-mad, ran in, closed before Ryder could get his hands up. Ryder lunged. Pumping solid punches to Sep Turnbull's midsection, Ryder forced him back. The man's face was puffed and heavily swollen; a split cheekbone drooled streams of blood. Ryder struck by instinct. The big fist powered straight to the other's jaw.

Sep Turnbull dropped like a shattered grain sack. Stretched on the ground, mouth and nostrils trickling strings of blood. Ryder reached, dragged an arm from beneath the man, straightened it.

Stomped. Stomped again. The brittle bones below Sep's elbow snapped.

One more. Ryder turned to Cady. The long, tall hardcase was still doubled into a horseshoe, but had managed to stop twitching. The man stared up at Ryder with fear-glazed eyes. "What ya gonna do?"

Ryder kicked his kneecap, heard it give with a crunch.

Pike Cady screamed.

Ryder picked up the black hat, jammed it on his head, made his way down the alley. The wagon was loaded with supplies. A bit stiff-limbed, he mounted the seat.

Out of town a mile, the big man fished in his vest pocket. One, two, three lucifer matches came to searching fingers. He brought them out.

Broken, every one.

Liz Kennesaw rocked on her veranda, Jenny Blake playing at her feet. The six-year-old's rag doll was scuffed and dirty, but she cradled it adoringly in her tiny arms and hummed a tune. From the railing beside the steps Ryder studied first the kid, then the lovely grown woman. The kid's face was content, Liz's haunted with some kind of melancholy. Did she miss her own child, Billy, now and for years past in the hands of his pa, Robeson? Mothers could be funny. Some would walk away from offspring without a qualm—as Liz seemed to have done. And then again, the motherly instinct, stifled, could come flooding back. Ryder had seen it before. Down in Sonora there'd been this peon family . . .

"Ryder?"

He shifted his position, let his leg down from the railing where it had hung cocked. A pleasant evening. Supper had been filling and delicious, another triumph for Sarah Blake as the new ranch cook. Now she was gone off with her husband on a stroll. Terry Shea was at the bunkhouse. Cathy and Jessica darned old socks in the parlor.

"Ryder, why are you doing it?" Liz's eyes were fixed on his swollen hands, the knuckles covered with cuts. "I mean, the fights in town. Terry tells me you leave your weapons at the ranch. Isn't that dangerous?"

"Oh, not too much." He sidled forward, careful not to disturb the kid's play. "Most folks don't cotton to gunning unarmed fellers. Can make it hot for those who do it. Robeson doesn't want the town against him. He's given orders to his men, I'm betting. So when them and me meet, we battle with our hands—plus our elbows and feet. Oh, things can get a mite rough-and-tumble, but—"

Liz interrupted. "All right, that's a part of my question answered. Has what I told you the other

165

morning got something to do with it?"

"That Robeson's riled and here in Texas on account of you? Yeah, Liz, it does. Maybe back at the beginning if you'd told Joe Kennesaw about your past, things could have been settled peaceable. Or at least more peaceable than they turned out. Killing breeds killing. I don't like to kill, though I seem good enough at it. I had a bellyful of killing in the War."

"So?"

"So, I'm trying to get at Robeson a new way. All his hands ain't hardcases. He's hired some away from the Rocking K, others signed on from ranches around the county. Terry Shea says the gunsels, those that didn't cash in in raids, only number six. I've put three out of the way with busted bones. That leaves three."

Liz's hand toyed with Jenny's flax-pale hair. "You believe that when the last of those are laid up, Richard will talk terms?"

"He won't have much choice. Next time in Yorktown, tomorrow, most likely, I aim to send some telegrams. There's friends of mine might be willing to come, work for you ladies. I'm talking about men good with guns as well as cattle. With the Slash-Diamond-Slash army busted up, the Rocking K full of piss-and-vinegar fresh hands— well, problems could be settled."

"Cathy and Jess and I won't have to clear out."

"That's the idea."

His face was hidden by the crescent shadow of the black hat. She reached up to him, stroked his cheek. "Thanks, Ryder."

166

"Well, I got to be heading for the bunkhouse. Orders for Shea. Plus turning in early. Tomorrow'll be busy."

Liz Kennesaw watched the big man cross the moonlit yard. She'd drawn the Blakes' child to her lap, and was rocking.

"Take them over to the blacksmith's, Shea. He'll know what to do. Me, I'm for the telegraph. As soon as my wires are on their way, I'll be joining you."

"Right." Ryder watched Shea lead the big bay, no longer lame, up the street in tow with the scruffy *grulla* he'd ridden. He shook his head at the change in the man. A week ago Terry Shea had been the scourge of half-empty whisky glasses left on saloon tables, soggy cigars from spitoons. Now the Irishman walked tall, and looked the part of the better-dressed rangeman.

When he disappeared inside the cavernous doors of the smith's, the big man entered the telegraph office. Ten minutes later he emerged smiling, snapped a lucifer, discarded it.

If answers to his wires came soon, good. If not, well, his friends were known to move around some from time to time. He'd eventually try others.

Now for the smith's. He'd just skip the beer today, out of consideration for the dried-out Shea.

When he passed the jail he glimpsed Bat Claymore at his desk, head thrown back, mouth open. The sheriff was asleep. *Fitting*, Ryder thought. *Awake, the feller just wastes time anyways. And that open mouth, now, there's a damn good fly*

167

forage.

A minute later he was at the blacksmith's, pausing briefly at the big doors to listen. No clatter or hammering. The smith could be talking to Terry. Ryder could damn near feel the forge heat through the wall.

"Ho, smith? Shea?" It was dim within compared to outside, the main light coming from the cherry-coal-bright forge.

He kicked something. Began a detour around the low obstacle. His eyes rapidly adjusted to the darkness and swept the ground for a fresh look. A man! A sprawled-out, still man.

Terry Shea!

"So, Ryder, no six-gun, no li'l old short sword today either," said a voice from the shadows.

A huge form loomed over Ryder like a wind-flagged tree. Worse, two more forms joined the first, both equally large, clutching equally heavy sledgehammers in hog-hock fists.

"Got no weapons, Ryder? Too bad!"

"*We* never signed no pledge promisin' you a square chance! Hell, we can't even write!"

"Now, just a damn minute, fellers!"

"For openers, we're Burl Anderson, Clem Q. Hotchkiss and Gato Mendez. Slash-Diamond-Slash riders one and all, proud as hell to work for Mr. Robeson."

Ryder took a step back. Came up with his shoulder blades flattened against the wall.

"Shit, Burl, that's enough palaver! I say pound the bastard."

All three giants charged.

CHAPTER 15

Ryder peered left, right, up and down with a quick sweep of his head. Although the gray eyes were growing more accustomed to the deep gloom inside the blacksmith shop, what they saw gave little comfort. He was backed to the wall, and one of the great, hunch-shouldered Slash-Diamond-Slash hands was making damn sure to stand between Ryder and the door. On the floor beyond Terry Shea's crumpled form stood anvils of various sizes. Across the room, the bay and *grulla* stood quietly tied, tails flicking at bluebottles.

At the end of the building's single room the forge was dimmer now, doubtless needing bellows work to fan its heat. Along the sidewalls sat stacked boxes of horseshoes, kegs of nails. One lidless barrel held only tools. Tools like sledgehammers.

The head of a nine-pound sledge whizzed inches from Ryder's nose. He could feel its wind. "You're cornered, Ryder!" Burl Anderson yelled, pumping up the forge. "And don't you count on the smith comin' by, neither, to save your ass. He's over at the Palace. We paid him to stay there!"

Another swing of the sledge, another miss.

Playing cat-and-mouse? Perhaps that was Ryder's chance. Distract the bunch. Get them talking. At least, like Ryder, the trio wore no guns. "Y'know, Bat Claymore just might drop in."

"Sheriff Claymore? You hear that Hotchkees?" The accented speech of Gato Mendez came from back behind Burl. "The Cat"—the most dangerous of the crew, Shea had said. "Sheet, that Claymore, he more Robeson man than me!"

"Gato!"

"Yeah?"

"Take this!" Ryder dove, scooped his fingers in the dust and fine-crushed horsedung underfoot. Lifted, tossed. A handful for the two ugly, angry faces. Both men swore, dropped the hammers, thrust hands to their stung eyes.

"Son of a bitch!" Clem Q. Hotchkiss waded in, this time meaning business.

Ryder ducked under the sledge's arc to come up swinging. One fist slammed the giant's gut, the other his fiery whisker scrub. Teeth crunched through hot blood. Ryder grabbed the hammer handle, twisted. The heavy tool came away in his hands.

Gato moved with speed worthy of his name, kicking the weapon out of Ryder's hands. Wrenched, flared pain, Ryder powered in anyway, launching a flurry of blows, lefts and rights, to the head of the breed. A cut opened along one high cheekbone, spurting crimson that subsided to a

170

drool. Lunging, Gato retaliated, blocked Ryder's uppercut, countered with a cross. The lightning blow slammed the big man's shoulder, producing pain, then an instant later, numbness. Ryder's arm wanted to drop, but he forced it up and at the breed. A stomach punch jackknifed Mendez. Ryder raised a knee to crash a nose. Gato mewed.

Crabbing sidelong, Ryder made room and the big breed dropped like a stone over a cliff. Now for Hotchkiss. Hotchkiss flung a horseshoe straight at Ryder. Ryder dodged, the hunk of iron thunking the wall behind, but by then the adversaries were licked in a clinch. Hotchkiss threw blow after blow into Ryder's body, but none hurt. Then gigantic hands closed on Ryder's throat. Ryder's head went light and sizzled with pain as he found his sight blurring. Helpless, he gasped.

Hotchkiss levered. Levered again. Ryder's flailing fists sought the enemy's head, but couldn't connect. Then he *did* connect, and heard a grunt. Ryder reached again, gouged, felt his fingers rake clear of skin in a welter of blood. He brought his arm around in a backward swipe. Knifing pain jolted his elbow, but the elbow found a voicebox.

There was a crackling, snapping noise, and Hotchkiss' arms fell away and Ryder was free. He spun, saw his opponent's face a bloody mask.

The fight had moved to the central floor area of the smithy. Hotchkiss was backed against a horse. Ryder moved in. The spooked *grulla* bucked and kicked. An iron-shod hoof met the small of Clem Hotchkiss' back and the man went flying.

Ryder tripped him. He went face down in a pile

of bright, new horseshoes and lay still.

"Goddamn son of a bitchin' bastard!"

Burl Anderson was flourishing rod-hot pincers!

Ryder froze, arms outstretched, watching the giant in front of him turn from the forge with the dangerous tool. He advanced, snarling.

Legs still rubbery from Clem Hotchkiss' ringnecking, Ryder moved back. Playing for time, a short time, any amount of time. Anderson swung the closed pincers like a scyth. The glowing end whipped past Ryder's nose reeking hot-metal smoke. Ryder reached to the side, swept a three-foot two-by-four plank into his grip. Now he swung. Wood met steel. Dueling, the men advanced, retreated. Ryder found himself backed between a pair of anvils.

Big Burl overhanded a powerful blow with the glowing pincers. Glancing an anvil, they sent a shower of sparks flying. He ducked Ryder's guard with the hot steel, scorching his shirt, and searing his skin. Ryder roared and hurled his club.

The club met the soft flesh of unprotected groin. Burl yelled. Ryder powered a roundhouse uppercut from near the floor. Anderson catapulted, his leg caught, trapped by an anvil. The thighbone gave with a mighty *crack*, and Burl Anderson's mouth opened in a scream. Then he was down.

Ryder vaulted over the man, and just in time.

"Hijo de puta," the half-breed rasped. *"Cabron!"* The man's hands moved rattler-quick, suddenly both held knives. As Terry Shea had described, a broad blade and a narrow blade.

All Ryder had to use were two bare hands.

172

The stalk was on. Gato Mendez, showing black and broken teeth, came in a crouch, both knives extended. Ryder took a step back, then a second. The man-cat's nose was skewed over to the side from Ryder's earlier blow, still leaked blood in substantial quantity. A weak spot. Another weak spot could be the balls, but to inflict damage there Ryder would need to get past the waving knives. Ryder flexed his fingers. His left hand remained numb, his right scuffed, bruised, painful. He made fists with effort.

Mendez leaped in, slashed but missed. He made a stabbing move with his left blade, but again didn't connect. All the time poised on the balls of his feet, Gato was never still, just kept shuffling, weaving, crossing, recrossing the floor by the forge. Ryder rushed, but wa fended off by the stiletto. He edged in the other direction, but Mendez slowly brandished the Bowie. Ryder longed for the feel of his chopped sabre. This business of not wanting to kill—it just might now get him killed.

"Keel you Ryder," Mendez hissed. "And Meester Robeson, his hundred-dollar bounty on you, gonna buy me plenty mescal!"

Bounty? Robeson? Son of a bitch!

Gato lunged, whipping the Bowie up and around, slicing Ryder's sleeve. Just a shallow cut on the arm, though a lot of hurt, some blood. But Ryder had exchanged positions with the breed, and now felt dry heat baking his backside. The forge! Hell, forced into it, he'd be in a fix!

Gato speared. Ryder backed. Now the warmth

173

of the coals was licking his rump, heating the rivets in his jeans. To turn this to advantage would take some doing. How?

Gato jabbed with his stiletto. Another crimson splash bloomed on Ryder's shirt.

The big man, off-balance, met the forge with his buttocks, the hot fuel-box ridge scorching deep, launching him forward again in a low, long dive. Ducking under the blades, Ryder circled the breed's waist with his arms and hugged grizzly-tight. Locked together, the two men whirled, and before the breed could use his weapons, Ryder flung him at the forge.

Gato Mendez dropped the knives, thrust his hands out to block his fall. Both hands raked deep into the live searing coals, fingers outstretched, probing. A loud sizzling sound, a stench like branding day filled the smithy. And the screams . . .

Robeson's bounty hunter flung free of the coals bed and stumbled. Outthrust in front of him were two charred-black hunks of meat, skin and sinew sloughing off, white bone. The breed toppled, screaming onto the filthy floor.

"W-what the devil's up?" Terry Shea stood on legs that swayed slightly, one hand pressed to the goose-egg on his temple.

"Ruckus. Done with now." Ryder was having trouble with the horses. They'd get shod another day.

"Them bastards clubbed me. Jesus, it hurts!"

"Figures."

Outside, mounted, riding up the main stem,

174

Ryder turned suddenly to the man on the *grulla*. "Terry, you reckon I'm worth a hundred, laid low, pounded to shit like Robeson wants?"

Shea grinned in glee. "You bet your ass!"

CHAPTER 16

"Now brace yourself hard. This might smart."

Smart, hell! When Liz daubed his cut cheek Ryder twitched involuntarily. The salve, boiled pine pitch mixed with rum was already laved generously over his torn knuckles and various burns, and stung almost as badly as the wet gunpowder poultice tied against his knife-gashed forearm. Where was the woman getting these remedies? She claimed her pa had worked with medicine up in Kansas, helping out other homesteaders. He had to accept that.

Anyhow, the treatment provided the best excuse for enjoying the attention of three of the handsomest young ladies Ryder had ever had the pleasure of. Plus a handsome older lady. Sarah Blake must have had a dozen years on the Kennesaw widows, but clearly would have been their equal in her girlhood. Blake seemed to appreciate the fact. The burly former saloonman sat on a milking stool in the kitchen's corner, his eyes seldom straying from his wife.

Another fine meal of steak, snap-beans and corn

would be on the table in minutes. Ryder's mouth, battered as it was, watered expectantly. He grinned at Terry Shea, himself under expert care as Jessica swathed his battered head with bandage.

"Lordy," Cathy Kennesaw was saying, hands laden with ointment jars and torn lengths of cloth. "You say those three bushwhackin' jaspers of Robeson's come out worse than you boys did in the fight?"

"By a far piece," Shea said. "Oh, Ryder got cut up some by Gato Mendez, but you ought to've seen the Cat. Plumb horrible, them burnt hands. It's gonna be a long spell before he uses a knife again, even to cut his grub."

"And the one called Burl?"

"Anderson? Bust-leg Anderson? Oh, I give him three-four months to get walking again without a crutch. Hotchkiss'll be laid up about the same time."

The blonde wagged her head. Jessica stepped back smiling. "There! Don't he just look pretty?"

"Pretty like some furriner in a—"

"Turban?" Ryder answered. Liz was finishing up with him, too.

"Yeah, one of them." She set her salve jar on the table and climbed to her feet. The long spill of auburn hair brushed his face. Accidentally? "The dressings on those worst burns will require changing. Ryder, you'll sleep in the house tonight. The spare bedroom."

"Whatever." He was grinning. Liz Kennesaw was brusque and businesslike. She sloshed water out of the tin pail by the washstand, went at her sticky hands with soap.

"How 'bout me?" Terry Shea said. "Bunkhouse gets powerful lonesome."

"Ryder isn't staying at the house for social reasons. His wounds could turn serious. The bump on your head ain't!"

"Yes, ma'am! No call to get ornery!"

Gus Blake, over in his corner, chuckled into his hand.

"Soup's on!" Sarah called, setting a huge china bowl on the table with a flourish.

It seemed Ryder had just gotten to sleep when the thud jarred him. Popped-open eyes showed him Liz. The redheaded widow had set a low-wicked lamp on the night stand, and was already unloading handfuls of jars. Above her scoop-necked flannel night shift, glistening hair cascaded to her shoulders. The full, generous lips seemed unusually pink tonight. Ryder wondered if she'd touched them with rouge.

"Ryder, I'll be right with you." On slender bare feet she padded to the door. Swung it closed, threw the bolt. Returning, she tugged the spare bedroom's one chair from the wall, placed it close by the bed, and sat down. "There." Her smile was slight, seeming modest.

"Er, come to give the patient his change of dressings?"

"Among other things. First I'd like to talk."

Ryder hadn't shaved since morning. His chin felt file-rough to his stroking palm. "Oh?"

"Yes. You've done so much for me and my

179

sisters-in-law. I don't believe I've thanked you enough. Oh, don't say you're just earning pay! I hired you, true, but the risks you're taking go beyond what money buys in this world. Look at these injuries you got today."

"Don't got to look. I can feel them right smartly."

"You make jokes. But honestly, Ryder, your bravery, that crazy sense of honor you carry around. Since you think I'm partly responsible for Robeson's rage, you took it on yourself to put his men out of action without killing them." She shook her head. The wonder in the smoky blue eyes seemed real.

What could Ryder do but shrug?

Liz went on. "I've learned a lot in these last days. A lot about courage, a lot about caring. The Blakes showed me, especially Sarah. The love she lavishes on her Jenny, it makes one think hard about being a mother. What it means. Ryder, do you have any family?"

"Mine died when I was a younker. Shot during a bank hold-up. Standing in line to make a deposit. After that an uncle raised me, but there was no love lost between us."

Liz nodded solemnly. "It's just awful to be without blood kin who care."

She paused for a long while. Ryder figured she wasn't about to continue, figured he knew what she was driving at anyhow. "Shoot, you don't need to say more about it, Liz. I reckon I understand."

"You *do*, don't you? You really do understand what I'm saying. Oh, thank you, Ryder! Thank you for that on top of all the rest!" And she was kissing him. Fingers wrapped in his thick black hair, her own hair spilling forward in a shiny auburn tent.

"Liz."

"Don't say anything." Her voice mumbled, her hands shook. As they strayed to the ribbon at her bodice and slowly loosed the little knot.

The dimity-lace neckline fell open in a vee. Liz Kennesaw shrugged sleeves from her milky shoulders, let the garment sip from her and stepped from fallen folds. Twin high breasts jutted in brown-tipped splendor. The waist was narrow, the muff at her triangle deep auburn.

"Jesus!"

"Don't say anything, Mr. Andrew Ryder. I figure you've been through plenty. I figure I owe you for helping out the Rocking K. Let me make a payment." With this she leaned forward under the glowing lamp, tossed the quilt that covered him aside. Beneath it he was naked.

"My God! I glimpsed you in the bathtub and you seemed normal-sized."

"I won't hurt you, Liz."

She enclosed him with her palm. Her spidering touch went to his mushroom head and it blossomed. He reached up, pulled her to the mattress and stroked a nipple. In a split-second it was bullet-hard, the surrounding aureole tightly puckered. Her tallow-slick thighs pressed against him hotly. She was trembling now.

She threw herself at him, falling across the sinewy chest, pressing pillow softness to banded muscle. It hurt his burns, but his response was quick. Wrapping a hand in the red curls, he pulled Liz's face to his own stubbled one, covered her warm mouth with kisses till she answered with her probing tongue.

"I want you in me! Now!"

Ryder's finger roamed, found her pleasure-tab. Warm, soft, pulsing, and now flooded with slick juice. Heaving over her, Ryder poised his manhood. She moaned, "Yes! Oh! Yes!"

His penetration burrowed deep, deeper, the sensitive tip of his powerful maleness savoring each hot inch. When he bottomed, the woman writhed like a skewered fish. Launching forward with still more power, he slammed against her again and again, the sharp *whap* sounds drowning bed creaks. She met each stroke with equal power, the sweet motion of it wild with passion.

"Christ, gal," Ryder found himself spouting, the waves of pleasure tossing him like a kite in a gale, his long stalk buried to the hilt. A keening cry of delight rose from the woman, and Ryder clasped her buttocks, holding her to him. Back arched, filled to overflow, Liz Kennesaw spasmed, then spasmed a second glorious time. His incredibly still-firm cock thrust, pulled, thrust in pliant rhythm. Approaching orgasm made the woman wild. She writhed, squirmed, bucked.

"Oh, God, Ryder. Yes! Yes!"

Liz's climax racked her, the vibrations centered at her love triangle nearly jerking her off the bed. Ryder joined in. Driving a final thrust to the depths of her, he felt the miracle begin again, the sudden first drops, then the flooding tide. She clasped him with her body, herself dazed at the power of her climax but wanting to give at the same moment. She wailed, screamed, fought. Then all at once she subsided, fell still, finished quickly as a mountain storm.

The fireworks gone out of him too, Ryder lapsed, flopping to the feather tick, gusting a sigh.

Ryder opened wide his half-shut eyelids. The woman was kneeling over him, his erection thrust like a turnstile bar between them. She grasped it, drew him close until, lifting with a smile, she nested that swollen, burgeoning part between her breasts. A drop appeared at his tip, and swaying slightly, she smeared the slick fluid along her skin, squeezing her mounds together with her palms to increase the pressure. Now both man and woman were breathing hard. Liz's nipples, miniature pebbles fused to satin, brushed the shaft of flesh, until, turning abruptly, she went to all fours.

"I've seen stallions do mares, Ryder! The way I feel, I could—"

"Any way you say, gal."

The big man got to his knees. The knob of him jabbed a buttock, slithered, then found target.

At her portal Ryder paused, savoring the caress of those wet, matted bush hairs. His entry, deliberate, slow, moved him inch by inch into her, each measured stroke a trifle deeper than the last. He dug kneecaps into the mattress, steadied as he drove into her, slamming her rump. At last he had penetrated totally and, holding that way, let the sweet pulsations of pleasure inundate him.

Low mumblings spilled from her: She dug in,

pushed back, then the gyrations started, rapid side-to-sides, exquisite, delicious. As the frenzy built, Ryder, hands under her body and at her breasts now, speeded his pace. Pendulum-like, the luscious pair jounced in his palms. Somehow the woman had managed to prop herself one-armed, and the feather touch of her fingers at her own mound sent new sensations coursing.

"Like this?"

"A little gentler . . . Please, Ryder. I-I do love it that way."

This orgasm sent shocks darting from her inmost recesses, her jammed cavity squeezed tight, clasping. She froze that way a brief moment as the wave of feeling crested and started to break. Man and woman poised in tableau, their forms lamp-washed, rosy, but then Ryder could wait no longer, withdrew almost to his bulb, then slid forward again, the last long plunge that poured spurt after spurt into her, lava-hot, torrential. "Yes! Yes!" Her cries had become half screams, uncontrolled, muffled in a bolster.

She slipped to the mattress. He, just as drained, joined her. The couple lay stone-still in a tangle of limbs.

"My God, Ryder!"

And her eyes closed, breaths dwindled, became slow, very regular.

Lulled, Ryder shifted, resting his bandaged forearm against her thigh. He didn't hurt so much. He felt utterly relaxed.

Within minutes, he, too, slept deeply, undreaming.

184

CHAPTER 17

"Goddamn son of a bitch! Where'd you say she's gone?"

Ryder stood over short Terry Shea outside the bunkhouse door. He couldn't believe his ears that early this morning Liz had ridden out.

"The Slash-Diamond-Slash, Ryder," Shea repeated. "Hell, I didn't know 'bout no trouble with your ears."

The big man spun on the heel of his stovepipe boot, strode for the corral, Shea barely keeping pace. "Oh, I heard you right the first time," he snapped. "Pea-brain notion for Liz to have, is all. Makes no damn sense!"

From a saddle on the ground, Ryder plucked a lariat. Eyeing the remuda on the other side of the corral poles through slitted eyes, he shook out a loop. Trouble was, he might have suspected something in the wind. Liz had seemed different last night when she'd visited him in his room. Spoke of his danger, his early days, motherhood, all dreamy-eyed, thoughtful. And the lovemaking— like there'd be no tomorrow.

His loop found the bay's neck, and once lassoed, the beast quieted quickly. Ryder led him to the barn, threw the blanket over the shining back, following with the saddle, the bags, rifle boot.

"Takin' your guns for a change, I see."

"Yeah, Shea."

"Takin' help, too?"

"Not you."

"Who, then?"

"Nobody. Goddamn it, *why'd* she go? Just when Robeson has got to cave soon?"

"She did mention Billy, but I can't guess what Robeson's son is to her."

Ryder gave the cinch a final tug, straightened the bridle. "Yeah, figures." Lifting boot to stirrup, swinging aboard. "Took her roan mare, did she? Rambunction?"

"Yep."

"Shea, I'll see you when I see you. Tell the others. But no one is to trail me, got it?"

"Got it."

He touched spur and the bay stepped out.

He only hoped his oversleeping didn't spell the end of things.

Ryder pushed the bay hard, the pulled fetlock now completely healed. The sun's blazing disk wasn't yet high and he'd just about covered half his journey. The Slash-Diamond-Slash lay due east of the Rocking K, nearly ten miles, two hours in the saddle.

Dust speared the sky ahead. Somebody was coming on a running cayuse. Funny, near here he'd met Shorty on the road and put the Robeson man to his last encounter. Maybe he'd do things differently this time, get the hell off the road, out of sight.

The last thing Ryder needed was delay in getting to Liz's side. He reined over toward a wash that sloped downward to his left. Close by the wash stood a dead lone tree, branches black claws against the sky.

The resolve to curb killing by now long gone from him, Ryder unleathered the Smith & Wesson. Broke the nickel-plated weapon open, checked its load. All good. Then he slid the six-gun loosely back in its holster. The rider was really near now, hoofs a-drum as the horse topped the rise.

Great God, the oncoming rider was no enemy— it was Liz. Liz with clothes ripped half off, rump high, head low, tied face-down across the saddle. The mare, Rambunction, spooked and galloping.

Clamping sharp rowels to the bay's flanks, the big man shot up the slope. Veering toward the runaway, he urged his gelding with whipping rein ends, the harsh, hot wind punishing eyes, cheeks, mouth. He'd misjudged distance. The charging bay was coming onto the road two lengths behind.

The bay swerved now, letting Ryder see Liz. Her long hair swept the ground, dust flying from the pounding hoofs. She'd slipped. Ryder could swear he'd seen the bonds holding her give at the saddle.

They drew closer. The roan was tiring. The bay, leggy, strong, a bit of Morgan in him, now made his most powerful move yet. Lashed and spurred, the animal gave its all and pulled slowly, painfully alongside. Ryder leaned over, but not far enough. He stretched out a desperate hand. Rambunction's bridle was only out of reach by inches. One inch, a half . . .

Caught it! Ryder clutched the leather headstall, and with a heave dragged the surging head down. The tall roan was slowing. Kicking and plunging, it dropped to a lope, a trot, then stopped. Ryder jumped to the ground and ran to Liz. He drew the short sabre and the blade slashed ropes.

"You all right, Liz?" She slid from the saddle into his arms quivering, but alive. He lowered her gently.

On the ground Liz curled into a ball, shaking violently, helplessly. In the prairie's hot stillness Ryder heard the chatter of her teeth.

"Liz! Liz!"

He still held the roan's reins looped in an elbow crook. Now he rose, pulled a pair of hobbles from the saddlebag and made quick work of confining Rambunction's forelegs. The woman was settling down, but he could see she didn't look good. Looked like hell, in fact. She was scared out of her wits.

Plus, she'd been beaten.

Liz Kennesaw's face was a mass of bruises. A mouse under her left eye had turned her entire cheek dark purple. The cuts and scrapes looked like the work of fists.

"R-Ryder?" she said, lifting that fine head from the dust.

"It's all right now. You're going to be all right."

"I—"

188

"Did this happen at Robeson's? Did that bastard . . ." He stopped talking. The woman's eyes had welled with quick hot tears.

Ryder stretched out his hand and touched her. She cringed. "Gal, you're safe now I'm with you. Want like hell to keep it that way. That's why I need to know if it happened at the Slash-Diamond-Slash?"

She looked up. Her cupid's-bow mouth had become an ugly gash. Now it twisted as she fought to get the words out. "I-I've been raped."

"Who? Robeson?"

Liz Kennesaw laughed, a strange sort of laugh that held contempt. "Richard? One thing I learned at his house, Richard Robeson cannot perform. Leastways not with a woman. There were men there, in the house, I mean, besides the punchers going about their work. One was Kyle, from Yorktown."

"Did Jason Kyle rape you?"

She was talking clearer, less shakily as anger grew in her. She half-shouted it. "No! After I'd told Richard I wanted Billy with me, he knocked me down and kicked me between the legs."

Ryder's teeth ground. "Go on."

"This stranger came in the room. I'd never seen him before, he seemed new at the ranch. A slight man, thin. He wore two six-guns, but he took them off, hung them on a chair, then—" The tears returned, this time overflowed, streamed down her cheeks. Seemingly acting by themselves, her hands clutched her shirt. She couldn't make the remnant cover her breasts. "Afterward, he and

189

Richard beat me. Like a team, almost, taking turns. I thought they'd kill me. Kyle brought Rambunction up to the back door. They tied me to her, then fired a shotgun to make her bolt."

Ryder scanned the sky. Time was flying. "If you can ride, I'll take you to the Rocking K. Cathy and Jess will take care of you, while I—"

"No! I mean, if you're going to Robeson's, I must come too. My visit shook Richard. He wants to keep Billy from me, claimed the boy was too sensitive to endure my troublemaking. Anyhow, he's having Kyle take Billy someplace. On the stagecoach. East, maybe. So I won't find him."

Ryder puzzled. "Let me get this straight. You want your son now, all of a sudden?"

"Not so sudden. The talks you and I had, Ryder, last night, even before—"

"You're sure about this, now, Liz? And you can ride?"

She put her legs beneath her and rose shakily. An ankle gave way and she caught at the big man. Then she seemed to steady. "Yes, I'm sure. But we've got to move fast. They were packing Billy's things, Kyle and the Angel."

Ryder had been striding to where the bay stood rein-thrown. At her words he froze. "The Angel?"

She was busy brushing dirt from her jeans. She peered across the distance between them. She had her color back, but looked tense, hair-trigger touchy. She pronounced the name carefully. "James Angel. I heard Richard call the new man that. He's ugly. His breath's sour. The hair on his head is all lank and greasy. Likes to hurt people."

"You said he packed two six-guns. Matched .45 Colts?"

"I'm not sure. Why?"

Ryder had the hobbles off Rambunction, now held the roan and the big bay short-reined. "Heard of the feller. Leastways if it's the same one. Jimmy Angel. Jimmy the Angel. The Angel."

"So?"

"Appears Robeson has bought himself a gunfighter. A fast one and deadly. The one that beat Kid Yuma."

She blanched. "My God! Then, Ryder, I can't let you go."

"I'm in this, Liz. For what they done to you, aim to do to Billy. Robeson, Angel, they got to be stopped!"

Then slowly, engagingly, Ryder grinned. "Anyhow, Kid Yuma, he wasn't so fast."

When they'd mounted, Ryder saw Liz controlling her horse one-handed as she tried, without complete success, to hold her ripped shirt over her jutting breasts. The big man stripped out of his vest quickly, handed the garment across to her. "Wear this."

"What? Thank you, Ryder." She really seemed delighted.

"Only one thing," he said, wheeling the bay onto the road and toward Robeson's spread. "Matches in the pocket. Don't lose them."

The pair exchanged smiles, and moved out.

"Hell!"

"What is it, Ryder?"

He'd been standing tall in the stirrups, scanning back along the road he'd come. Now he grunted disapproval. "There's folks on our backtrack. I don't like it."

"Why?"

"Who could it be? Too far back now to see much but dust, but they're sure riding hell-for-leather."

She, too, had reined her horse around, and now shaded her eyes with a hand, squinting. "I must not see what you see."

"Try this trick the Comanches use. Make a roof with your locked fingers, look out under it. Sharpens the view."

"It works! Say, looks like they're getting closer. More than one rider, more like three or four. And coming hard."

"May as well wait for them. That pinto in the lead, I've seen Jessica riding him to work cows. It's got to be the gals, and likely they've brought Shea and Blake with them. I told that pair not to follow me."

Ryder shrugged. He couldn't be too angry. One of the worries that had started to nag him did concern Liz. She didn't really belong in the thick of the fray when he came on Robeson. In the hands of her sisters-in-law, Liz would be just fine.

Shea, Blake and the women pounded up after a few minutes.

"Back there I told 'em what you said, Ryder, but Miz Jessica, she wouldn't be stopped."

"Ryder," Jessica put in, "how could you try to cut every one but you out of the action. Liz! Your face! Your clothes!"

"What happened?" Cathy urged the steeldust gelding she straddled in past the others and close. Deep lines of concern bracketed her mouth.

"I'll tell you . . . " And Liz started to do so. Ryder, meantime, sized up the Rocking K arsenal.

"You boys brought plenty of guns?"

"We are each packin' two Winchesters," Gus Blake observed, "plus a couple six-guns apiece. Hell, them and all the shells—"

"Were my idea," said Terry Shea. "Didn't see no hardware goin' with Miz Liz this morning. Maybe if she had they would be hurting, not her." In a lower voice he questioned, "The boss-lady, she all right?"

"Will be. Thanks, Shea."

Ryder surveyed his crew, found little wrong. The set of Gus Blake's jaw spoke of loyalty, readiness to fight. Shea, the Irishman, obviously awaited his chance. "Let's ride!"

Over the next rise lay Richard Robeson's Slash-Diamond-Slash. Occasionally the bark of a dog drifted on the breeze.

"You women'll wait here," Ryder snapped. "Me, Terry and Gus will go in after the younker."

"What younker?" Cathy wanted to know.

"Billy."

"What Billy? Billy Robeson? I don't understand."

"I'll explain," Liz said. Immediately she had her two sisters-in-law grouped in horseback conference.

"That what we're here for, another kidnap-

193

ping?" Terry Shea's brow curled in a frown.

"That's not all. This Robeson's the lowest sidewinder in Texas. Turned his gunsel loose on Liz, and he hurt her bad. I aim to get even for the lady. The only problem could be that same feller, called Angel."

"Angel?" Gus queried.

"He's a gunslick, from out Pecos way. Robeson must've wired for him when I was out-fighting the likes of Burl and Gato. Angel just got in."

Shea wagged his head. "So, what do we do?"

"Ride straight into the Slash-Diamond-Slash yard. Me in the lead, you two sprgad out, carbines on saddle bows. When we get to the house, I'll call out the Angel. You boys will get the drop on the punchers."

Blake and Shea gave grim nods in unison.

"Move out."

"Lordy, lieutenant, you been outa the cavalry how long?"

Ryder grinned, moving out and up the slope. Not showing the grin to Blake. The threesome topped the rise and started down. The main house looked even bigger in daylight. If Robeson didn't appear, Ryder aimed to ride right up the front steps.

As they crossed the yard a few punchers glanced up from their chores. Some sets of eyes narrowed. No guns in view.

At the foot of the mansion Ryder reined in. "Robeson! Angel!"

Slowly, the door behind the pillars opened. A figure stepped forth, rail-thin, loose-jointed. The man wore no hat, and the lank hair that streaked his forehead was the color of brown mud. The eyes, cold black disks, fixed on Ryder with deadly intensity.

Each delicate hand brushed a six-gun butt.

"I'm Angel. You got to be Ryder. Welcome to your funeral."

CHAPTER 18

My funeral? Ryder smiled. Of course, Jimmy the Angel was trying to get the edge right off by saying that to him. Strike some kind of fear into his heart. But Ryder's heart didn't know the kind of fear a man like Angel might cause. He might fear Comanche torture, or the agonizing death of a rattler bite. But a man like Jimmy Angel provoked too much rage. The bastard had to be battled and beaten, and in this task, fear had no part.

Ryder studied his antagonist. Everything he'd ever hated in a man seemed combined in this individual before him. Arrogant. Cold-blooded. A killer who enjoyed killing. Or maiming. The kind of man without a shred of moral fiber. A glint of intelligence lit those black eyes. Here wasn't someone stupid like Hotchkiss, Cady, Burl. Angel could earn a living in a profession, but instead had turned hardcase.

All five-feet-two inches of his stature, all one-hundred-and-twenty pounds of the little bastard were mean.

From a corner of his eye Ryder glimpsed Robeson emerging from the house to stand next to the door. The man with hair like burnished tin looked tired. He didn't raise his gaze from the porch floor.

"Angel, I'll deal with you later. First I want to talk with Robeson."

"You won't be talking after I—"

"It's all right, Jimmy." Robeson's voice was clear but gruff. "Ryder, I guess I know the reason you're here. Dismount, come inside for a drink. I'll persuade you yet that my former wife—"

"I'm here on account of your son," Ryder broke in.

Robeson shrugged. "Dismount. I don't enjoy looking up at horsemen, even from a porch."

Ryder saw Shea and Blake posted as directed. They sat their horses between the house and bunkhouse, rifles cocked, ready. None of the hands standing about moved.

"I reckon I will." Ryder lifted in his stirrups, swung down off the bay. He advanced through the dust of the yard, spurs chiming softly. When he reached the foot of the mansion steps he started up.

"Hold it!" Jimmy the Angel's mouth was twisted, his breathing fast. The cords in the hands were taut as banjo strings.

"Jimmy, it's all right, I'll go down to him." This Robeson did, step by cautious step. "There now," he said when he faced the big man across three feet of hoof-stirred yard dirt. "That's much better. Tell me, Ryder, what about my Billy?"

Ryder edged his voice with steel. "There was a disagreement about him here this morning."

"With Liz, the whore that's the boy's mother. Yes, she did stop by. And I made her the same offer I've made so often in the past. That she return to me."

"To live as wife?"

Robeson nodded. "A wife to me, a mother to young Billy."

"She's scared of you, Robeson. And considering what happened today, she's got cause. But I aim to come back to that. Is the boy here?"

"He is."

"But won't be for long. When does Jason Kyle leave with him to catch the stage?"

"Look, Ryder, Billy Robeson is her son, did she tell you that? Did she mention how she abandoned us both up in Kansas? That she found her wifely duties too much of a burden?" Richard Robeson's face flooded with hate. A vein twitched in his scrawny neck. "Did she describe the ingratitude to a returning soldier after four years of hell on battlefields? Did she, Ryder?"

"There's a difference in your versions, Robeson. You know, you can believe this or not, but there was a time I tried to see your side. No more."

"She came here this morning to mock me!"

Ryder's lip curled. "I doubt she'd ever have got on the subject of wifely duties if you hadn't pressed yourself on her. But never mind that now. She wants the boy. The kind of man you are, ain't no telling what you'll make him into. So trot the kid out."

"Never!"

"You let your gunsel rape Liz. Helped him beat

her up. You're going to pay for that, Robeson, but the kid should be out of the way first." Ryder started up the steps.

"Jimmy!"

The Angel's hands streaked for his big Colts. Rumor was right, they were a matched pair, and both cleared leather as quick as a rattler strikes. Ryder's gun hand moved lightning quick, bringing up the Smith & Wesson. Jimmy triggered, firing from the porch. Missed. A .45 lead bee hummed by Ryder's ear. Simultaneously, the Angel's left-fist gun boomed. This slug tugged Ryder's sleeve.

The Angel's thumbs were earing his twin hammers back. The man was fast, but not accurate. Ryder's finger stroked his own gun's trigger just as it came level, an instinctive motion, long-practiced. Orange flame belched from the S & W's business end, and a hot slug slammed into the head of Angel above an eye. The face caved inward, the mouth twitched, and as the ball exited behind, brains and red blood splashed on the whitewashed walls.

"Christ!" Richard Robeson's yell was anguished, vengeful as he fled up the steps, awkwardly leaping over Angel's fallen corpse. He ran inside and slammed the door. Ryder heard a bar drop. He tried the latch, but it refused to open.

But by then gunfire was volleying back in the yard. The big man spun on his heel, the Smith & Wesson still in his grip. Shea and Gus Blake were wheeling their horses in circles, firing randomly at punchers firing back. A bowlegged wrangler with a fierce red mustache triggered and dove headlong behind a rain barrel. Two slugs ventilated it. It spouted water.

Ryder vaulted down the steps and ran. To his right stood the bunkhouse. The glass pane crashed, broken from within, and a long pistol barrel thrust out, bloomed a puff of smoke. Gritty dust kicked at Ryder's boot, but he didn't stop sprinting. Colliding with the wall, he fetched up. The window just to his left crashed. The muzzle of a Winchester appeared, swung in an arc to draw a bead on Gus Blake. Ryder grabbed the rifle, yanked. Luke Cord's head and two brawny arms came over the sill with the gun. Ryder clubbed the hardcase to the back of the neck. Cord disappeared inside.

Twin barrels of a Greener ten-gauge blasted by his head, searing his cheek, bringing blood to his ears. Behind him, Ryder heard a horse and, then he saw Terry Shea's mount go down, a hideous side wound spilling gore. Shea catapulted clear, rolled over twice, came up with his brand-new peacemaker. Threw a shot.

Out of the bunkhouse window beside Ryder Sep Turnbull pitched, mop of hair bloodied, an extra eye blown in the face where a nose belonged. And they kept coming. Clem Q. Hotchkiss brought his Army Remington to bear.

Ryder shot first. The slug plowed the barrel chest, devastated lungs and heart to send a great welter of crimson splashing shirt and sill. Fine red droplets splattered Ryder.

Shea pounded up, threw himself beside Ryder against the wall.

"Terry, you made it."

"I made it. Out there on a horse, I made too good a target. Now, if Blake'd only protect *his* ass."

Blake swung down from his black horse, lit a shuck for cover, belly-flopped behind a narrow tool shed. The red-mustached man reared from behind his barrel, took aim . . .

Terry Shea tossed a shot. Mustache's body jerked with the slug's impact. Blake turned, threw his Colt in the right direction, and blew his lights out. The man writhed for a moment and was still.

"Got 'im," Shea observed. "Most of 'em are inside, though. How 'bout this bunkhouse?"

Ryder pondered. "Big, dry as tinder. Shea, let's fire it!" He reached toward his vest. "No matches. Liz borrowed my vest."

"Hell, and *I* don't smoke! Wait! Look!"

Terry Shea pointed. Gus Blake, grinning, was coming out of his little hideout shed. Holding something aloft. Something round and red in color?

"Pritchard's Red Star, by the color! Dynamite, man! He's sizin' the bunkhouse!"

"He knows we're here?"

"Naw."

"Then, goddamnit, let's cut!"

"Wait! The women!"

And sure as hell, here they came, galloping full-tilt into the ranch yard, sweeping abreast past the pole corral, heading for the mansion. A volley of gunfire poured from the bunkhouse, one hardcase darting from the door to blaze away. He was dropped by Liz Kennesaw. The woman spurred past without a glance and disappeared out of sight behind the main house.

"What are they up to?"

Terry Shea elbowed Ryder's ribs. "What Gus Blake's up to's a better question for us!"

"Christ, the explosive!"

When they broke from the cover of the bunkhouse a yell went up. Ryder thought he caught the voice of Gato. Shea and Ryder pounded for the mansion, slugs singing past their ears, spanging dirt underfoot. Ahead, Jess and Cathy laid down fire, covering them. "Look out!" he yelled.

The explosion filled the air, and a wall of pressure swept Ryder and Shea off their feet. Their shirts were sucked at and there was heat. Thrown headlong, they met hard, dusty ground with their chests, bounded immediately up to run again. A crackle of flames came from the ravaged bunkhouse, some loud screams . . .

On the mansion steps they paused, turned. Sheets of fire tossed sky-high above the pile of shredded timbers that had been the bunkhouse. Jess and Cathy stood with faces chalky, guns in their hands, but numb. Gus Blake stalked across the yard toward them. Leisurely. Relaxed.

"Reckon that does it," Shea said.

Ryder was querying the women. "Why'd you ride up? What's Liz up to?"

"Billy," Jess said. "We were watching from the rise, saw everything. Saw you kill *him*." Grimacing, she indicated the sprawled body of Jimmy Angel. "Liz was afraid Robeson would get away

203

out the back. No one's seen him or Kyle."

True enough, no one had. And there was indeed a back door to the mansion. Ryder had exited by way of it himself the night he'd come here alone and snatched Billy. "Maybe we better take a look-see." He tried the front door, again, found it unmoving on the massive hinges. Picking up a cast-iron boot scraper from the porch floor, he flung it. The large plate window beside the door shattered.

"Now!" Ryder thrust head and shoulders through and surveyed the place. The window let into the large foyer where on his last visit he'd confronted Dutch and Hank.

They all climbed through, Ryder was first to throw a leg over the low sill. Cathy's and Jessica's eyes roamed the place, taking in the luxury of rugs, paintings, furniture. Shea looked beyond, peeking into the parlor. Blake scouted the hall to the rear. Nothing.

But neither Ryder nor his companions put up their six-guns. The smell of danger filled the place. Danger for Liz.

"She said she'd be going in the back way," Cathy whispered. "Try to surprise Robeson. She's good with a gun, I know, but—"

"Risky, I agree," Ryder said. "We better spread out, find her. Take the first floor first. Shea, that wing to the right, I never been in there, but that's space to cover. Blake, you want to try the north wing?"

"Will do."

"Me and the gals will try the kitchen. Ready,

Cathy, Jess?"

They were. Ryder led the way, the long-barreled Smith & Wesson preceding him at full cock. Though the flint-gray eyes darted from cranny to cranny as they moved along the hall, he knew the women were at his back. Tip-toeing.

There was no one in the kitchen, pantry or cellar. Not even a sign of life, but for a half-full whisky bottle on the massive table. Ryder shrugged at the women, snared the bottle by its neck before he retraced his steps. At the foot of the great staircase under the chandelier, the entire party reassembled. Neither Terry Shea or Blake had seen sign of Liz.

"That leaves the second story," Ryder told them. "Now, sure as hell, Robeson and whoever is up there with him know we're down here, and not just to view the art. They figure we'll be coming up. There's another way down, a back way, and I'm going to station Blake and Jessica by those stairs to block a retreat. Soon's that's done, Shea, me and you will go on up."

"What about me?" Cathy wondered.

"Good question. Gal, I want you to wait yonder, right out front. There's always a chance they'll use a window, try and make a break, or far drop to the ground. You got a gun. You got your lungs. If you want the rest of us to come a-running, shoot or holler."

She liked the idea of the chore. Twirling her six-gun's cylinder with a whiz of ratchet clicks, she stomped outside.

"All right, down that hall's the back stair, Blake.

You see the nook?"

Soon Gus and Jessica were at posts near the spot indicated. Six-guns in hand, read for action.

"Well, Terry?"

"You first, me first, or we move together?" The Irish grin on the little man's lopsided mug barely masked his tension.

Ryder glanced down at the whisky bottle he still held. He needed Shea, he needed Shea steady, as an extra gun he could absolutely count on, for five minutes. After that there'd be no matter. He thrust the bottle at his sidekick. "A drink?"

Sweat stood out on the brow of Terry Shea. The moist eyes glittered, a tongue as dry as the Mojave flicked lips of paper. Then the mouth stopped working and set firmly in a grim line. "Thanks, no. Never touch the stuff."

Ryder nodded, set the booze bottle down on the lowest step. "Then, let's go. Me first, you back me up."

They began their climb.

At the first landing Ryder moved against the wall, froze for a long minute listening. Then his waiting ear caught the sound of ragged breathing. Up above Richard Robeson waited, a ruined rancher who had watched his bunkhouse destroyed, his hardcase army killed from an upstairs window. This one would be vengeance-bent. He'd already been two-thirds loco on the visit of Liz this morning.

Liz was with the bastard. She had to be. She was certainly nowhere else to be seen. Her situation, the danger she might be in was something the big

206

man hated to contemplate. Yet contemplate it he must. If he was to save the woman, it would likely need doing in the space of a minute. No second tries, if Robeson held a gun to her head. No more tries at all.

A floorboard creaked. Ryder exchanged glances with Terry Shea. Past the long, gray-steel frame of his Colt, the Irishman winked.

No choice. Slowly, the pair climbed.

As the crown of Ryder's black hat crept level with the topmost step, a shot rang out. A small hole drilled in the black hat's crown, low, dead center.

Ryder reared, rushed up the last few stairs, hurling the decoy hat from his six-gun barrel to sail against the wall. He crashed into Richard Robeson, knocked him backward. The rancher slipped, went to one knee. "No, don't take Billy! Please!"

Liz was in the hall. Robeson had her, his hand wrapped tight in her loose, red hair. Now he drew her in front of him, a human shield.

"Son of a bitch," Terry Shea hissed from beside Ryder.

"Freeze, Terry. He's going to say something."

"You fooled me, Ryder, with that old hat trick," Robeson husked. "Congratulations. However, now, for all your fooling, you'll only get to see the woman die!" He held a tiny, Rupertus pepperbox at Liz's temple.

"And after the woman's dead," Robeson announced, "I'll see to *your* deaths! Haw!"

"Crazy as a loon!"

"But dangerous, Terry. Don't risk anything. Don't move."

"I'm sorry, Ryder," Liz moaned. "Robeson hid in a closet when I came upstairs. Got the drop on me."

A vicious jerk whipped the woman's head around.

Twisting violently, Liz Kennesaw stretched her arched neck out and down, and planted her row of straight, white teeth on Robeson's gun hand, to bite with all her might.

Ryder launched forward, followed by Terry Shea. Scrambled up and into the second-floor hallway, six-guns up, cocked. . .

The rancher shook the woman loose. She was hurled at Ryder. Shea snapped off a shot. It shattered a glass lamp chimney as Robeson dove through a doorway. A slug from Ryder gouged the jamb. "Is it where Billy's hid?" Ryder yelled.

"No!" Liz was on her feet. "Across the hall!"

Ryder ran to the room and tore the door open. The kid was there, looking pasty-faced with fright. His mother grabbed his arm, dragged him past Ryder toward the stairs.

Shea shouted, "Go in after Robeson?"

"Looks that way. Christ! What do I smell?"

"Coal oil! Smoke! Fire!"

The smoke was billowing under the door that Robeson slammed behind him. On the other side, the crackle of flames.

"Everybody out! The kid and Liz are clear. Jess and Blake, they got to be warned."

When they reached the foot of the staircase, Jess

and Gus Blake were already piling past. "Out-side!"

"Where's Robeson?"

"God knows! He fired his place! Used lamp oil. Feller's loco as hell!"

The women were waiting well back in the ranch yard. Cathy embraced Jessica, Liz Kennesaw wrapped her arms about her kid, Billy. As they watched the house a shadow darkened an upper window. Three seconds later Richard Robeson kicked out the glass.

The man balanced on the sill and laughed a high-pitched wail. Robeson's face wore cuts from glass. Grim-faced, snarling, lips peeled back from yel-low teeth, he launched a roar. He raised the Rupertus, pointed it at Liz, triggered. Triggered again.

Both balls fell miserably short, making minia-ture dirt-geysers where they hit ground. "Ryder! He's trying to kill Billy!"

Ryder, the cocked, shiny Smith & Wesson in hand, still held his fire. "He ain't got range with that pea-shooter."

Fire leaped high amid smoke from the house roof. The room behind Richard Robeson was a mass of flame. But things weren't over. From the side of the window another figure stepped, raising a six-gun, taking point-blank aim. At Robeson. The gun blazed.

The rancher, head-shot, staggered and fell back inside. The man jumped the sill, dark frock coat smoking, hit the porch roof, rolled, shot off the roof, fell through empty air screaming. He hit the

209

ground with a dull thud.

Ryder dragged Jason Kyle from under the collapsing wall. He stretched the fragile frame out straight in the deep dust.

"Why?"

"He shouldna brought in Angel." Kyle's voice was very weak. "Nothin' Angel could've done that I couldn't—"

His voice cracked, and he died.

CHAPTER 19

The day was another clear and dry one. The tall, wide dome of azure overhead seemed to hold the sun suspended. As the blazing white ball climbed toward its zenith, so did the heat, baking the ground's scant grass fringe to an even paler, brittler brown. It forced dogs to lie panting under porches. It drove cattle to stream banks, making them crowd for shade.

It popped sweat on the hides of Texans—and some others passing through.

Ryder swabbed his brow with his bandana. He stood between the Rocking K corral and barn, gray eyes squinting in the direction, due west. Three black dots had just topped the horizon, lofting dust plumes, and came for the ranch.

Horsemen.

Ryder reached a lucifer match from the pocket of his vest. Put it to his lips.

Out back of the smokehouse Shea and Blake were readying for roundup. From where he was Ryder could see heaped rope coils, chaps, tack, camp gear littering the ground. Beyond stood the battered chuck wagon, canvas bonnet ripped in many places, one wheel sporting at least two broken spokes. Lots of work to be done.

Now, with Robeson dead, the widows Kennesaw would be able to get on with their lives. But, to do so required money, the money a longhorn herd would bring at Abilene.

Money for gowns, furs, feathered hats. Money for train fare on the long trek east, back to St. Louis. Or Chicago. Or in the case of the sweet, blonde Cathy, home to green-hilled Tennessee.

If that was what the gals really wanted.

Ryder would be moving on to New Mexico Territory. His intended destination before his horse had been lamed.

The Rocking K folks came down off the veranda on the front of the house. Jessica, Cathy, and Liz. Liz's Billy, all smiles, a bit fatter now, bringing up the rear. A happy crowd, it seemed. Ryder grinned, waved.

Cathy pounded up on flying feet, threw her arms around the big man. A second later Jessica followed suit. When Liz reached him, she pushed high to tip-toe to plant a tender kiss smack on his mustache-curve. Finally, all the excited gals jumped back and clapped their hands.

"Ryder, tomorrow the roundup begins. We start the drive north on Tuesday week."

"Planned it out, have you, Liz?"

"Bet your boots! And with you ramrodding the herd—"

He removed the lucifer from between his teeth, studied it a moment, snapped it. Dropped the slivers of it in the dirt. "I ain't going with you."

"What?" They yelled together. Even young Billy Robeson looked bewildered.

"I got plans to be in Santa Fe before snow flies."

There was disappointment on their three lovely faces. Each woman cared for him, Ryder knew. Each had panted with him, wild with passion.

His saddle lay on the ground where he stood. Grinning, he hoisted it to his shoulder, shrugged the weight around till it was comfortable. The bay was watching from the corral, alert, recognizing him, ears forward.

"You don't aim to leave today?"

"Not before . . ."

Out of a corner of his eye, he saw spite crackling between the three young women. He spoke curtly. "No need to hang about."

"No need? There's our cattle drive!"

Down by the creek, three loose-jointed, range-brown riders were splashing across. Smiling, the leader raised a hand and tipped his sombrero brim. He had a square jaw, eyes as blue as a mountain lake. His *compadres* grinned too, the stocky young sandy-beard, the medium-build sorrel-head.

"Ladies," Ryder said, "meet some friends of mine. I sent out telegrams some time back about your troubles."

The newcomers reined in, towering on horse-back above the women, the boy, Ryder. All by now had swept their hats off. "this here's Bob Bosley," Ryder announced. The square-jawed man beamed. "And tall Cal Gideon. And on the end, Frank Phelps. All are top cow hands, in every way. Boys,

213

the Kennesaw widows."

Jess, Cathy, and Liz exchanged awed looks. These men were attractive. Downright handsome, in fact. All were vigorous, in the prime of life, slabbed with muscle.

"Ryder mentioned troubles," Jess Kennesaw squeaked shyly. He green gaze roamed the blunt face of Phelps. "But our troubles are over now."

"Leastways, gunplay troubles," Cathy explained. Or tried to, with eyes fastened on Cal Gideon's teeth. Strong, straight, pearly . . .

"But we do have some minor troubles to plague us, Mr., er, Bosley, is it?" Liz was fascinated by the curling tendril of hair that crept down Bob's brow. "You see, we got beef on the hoof, needs to get to the railroad."

"Shucks, I drove the Chisholm trail often." Bob Bosley's voice was rich and deep.

"Really? Well, the Rocking K sure is needing to sign on hands. If you and your pards see your way clear, there'll be work here—permanent."

Ryder strolled to the corral rails, swung down his saddle. Brought the bay out, readied it to ride. Mounted, he looked around, saw Bob, Frank, Cal standing talking to the Kennesaw gals. Standing close. Shea and Blake, curious, were strolling over. At the house, Sarah played with Jenny.

"Adios, folks. See you all down the trail, maybe."

"So long, Ryder."

"Be seeing you."

"Yeah, see you again. Further along the trail."

Ryder kicked the bay into a lope. Within minutes

the Rocking K buildings fell behind a rise.

This time when he fished a match to chew, he was grinning.

Saddle up with Ryder as he heads South of the
Border for some cold tequila and hot senori-
tas, only to be taken prisoner by a mangy
band of killers. They need his military exper-
tise to train them to fight—but the only lesson
they get is how to die when they tangle with
Ryder's lightning-fast gun in . . .

RYDER #3: RYDER'S ARMY